THE BEST AUSTRALIAN
STORIES

2017

THE BEST AUSTRALIAN
STORIES

20
17

EDITED BY MAXINE BENEBA CLARKE

Black Inc.

Published by Black Inc.,
an imprint of Schwartz Publishing Pty Ltd
Level 1, 221 Drummond Street
Carlton VIC 3053, Australia
enquiries@blackincbooks.com
www.blackincbooks.com

9781863959612 (paperback)
9781925435900 (ebook)

Cover design by Peter Long
Typesetting by Tristan Main

Printed in Australia by McPherson's Printing Group.

FSC
www.fsc.org
MIX
Paper from
responsible sources
FSC® C001695

Contents

Introduction

Maxine Beneba Clarke

Writing the perfect short story is like skimming a stone. There's the testing and selection of material: the running of thumb over smoothness of surface; the weighing of rock in palm. There's the framing of the story: the selection of angle and entry point, just so. The side-tilt of the body; the squint against the sun; the raising of the hand; the assessment of the water; the pace of the throw. The let-go. Then, after all these things have aligned into perfect overall technique, there's just that little bit of luck. How far will the stone travel? How many jumps will it make across the surface? How wide will the ripples be when it connects with water, and how deep will they run? And, at the end of it all, did it seem like just a casual throw?

Junot Díaz. J. California Cooper. Nam Le. Alice Munro. James Baldwin. Cate Kennedy. William Faulkner. David Malouf. The best short fiction writers place their pens down and leave you with a *haunting*: a deep shifting of self, precipitated by impossibly few words. The challenge, then, as an editor was to carefully locate those stories which so sung, among the hundreds upon hundreds of excellent stories encountered.

In Dominic Amerena's 'Help Me Harden My Heart', there is the sharp intake of breath as a handful of decades-old baby teeth are scattered across a kitchen; there is the gut-punch shock of vile words, spat from the mouth of a teenager who grew up alongside yours. Cassie Hamer's 'By Proxy' captures the overwhelming uncertainty of leaving home for unknown shores. This story is at once unique and universal. The mass movement of people around the world and the precarious position of women in such transits are both age-old issues and contemporary concerns. In Melissa Lucashenko's 'Dreamers', the author paints an unforgettable portrait of strangers, bound by love and loss to become family. Lucashenko's story is a masterful exercise in restraint, letting unspoken histories echo through. In Verity Borthwick's 'Barren Ground', we become uncomfortably complicit in the protagonist's uncertainty about saving the life of a person she has deeply loved.

These stories push and pull at our hearts, demanding entry into their chambers. These stories vary from the surreal to the naturalistic, from the satirical to the poignant, from loud declaration to murmured whisper. They are delivered by achingly familiar voices, and attached to author names I had never before encountered. They were published in leading Australian literary journals, anthologies and newer publications, or have not yet been published. Taken together, these stories also sing of the country that we are. Of our history, and our hopes; our battles and our dreams.

An Aboriginal woman storms into a hardware store, and demands an axe. A rickety boat quietly leaves the coast of Australia, carrying hopeful future-seekers of an entirely different demographic. A young boy leaves home on an ordinary day, and returns deeply and disturbingly altered. A trampoline is unexpectedly delivered one summer afternoon on the suburban lawn of a fractured family. The government builds a wall to separate the population, splitting one Australian home right down the centre. Bored country-kid neighbours string a makeshift walkie-talkie telephone between their bedroom windows. A bemused family unconditionally rallies around an unexpected but adored arrival. A schoolchild, unable to verbally articulate his trauma, encyclopaedically documents schoolyard happenings. A child of two worlds devastatingly splits himself in two, in order to negotiate hybrid identities.

This is how we wrote Australia. These are the best Australian stories from 2017.

Sissy

Tony Birch

Sissy had never been on a holiday and didn't know anyone at Sacred Heart School who'd travelled much further than the local swimming pool. At best they'd enjoyed a tram ride to the picture theatre in the city, maybe once or twice a year. A girl in the same year at school, Ruby Allison, who lived behind the dry-cleaners with her mother and two older brothers, came back to school after the holidays and told a story about how she'd been to the ocean that summer. Ruby sat in the schoolyard at lunch-time, a circle of girls around her, and talked animatedly about the giant waves and the seals basking on the rocks above the beach. No one else in the group had seen the beach and they had no reason to question Ruby's story. Except that she'd been seen most days helping her mother behind the counter in the oppressive heat of the dry-cleaning shop. If the story was untrue, and Ruby hadn't been near the sea, she'd displayed a vivid imag-ination, which was hardly surprising. If the girls from the school excelled at anything, it was storytelling. As Sister Josephine often remarked, *Those who have little or nothing have the greatest capacity for invention.*

Each afternoon, following the final bell, Sissy would walk to the House of Welcome on the main street, operated by the Daughters of Charity. She'd join a line at the front gate, queuing to collect a tin loaf of white bread, or fruit bread if she was early enough, and an occasional treat of biscuits, before heading home. She also attended Girls Club at the House on Saturday mornings. The sole reason Sissy's mother allowed her to join the club was that the morning ended with a mug of chocolate milk and a buttered roll, followed by a hot bath for every girl. Sissy didn't look forward to bath time. The girls were required to line up in alphabetical order and the bath water was changed only after the Ks – Sheila Kane and Doreen Kelly – had bathed, usually together for the sake of economy. Sissy was sure that more than one girl in the line ahead of her took a pee in the water, out of either spite or necessity. She'd spend all of thirty seconds in the bath, and never put her head under the water let alone wash her hair, which she preferred to do under the cold water tap over the gulley trap in the backyard at home, no matter how bitter the weather.

*

One Saturday morning, she was about to leave the House with Betty Reynolds, her closest friend. Sister Mary, who ran the club, took Sissy aside and asked to speak with her. Although she couldn't think of anything she'd done wrong, Sissy worried that she was in trouble. She asked Betty to wait for her out front of the House and went and stood outside Sister Mary's office door. The nun occasionally looked at Sissy over the top of her steel-rimmed glasses as she wrote in an exercise book. When she had finished, Sister Mary closed the book, picked up an envelope, opened it and read over the details of a typed letter.

'Come in, Sissy,' she said.

Sissy stood in front of Sister Mary and looked down at the navy-coloured habit covering the nun's head. She wondered, as she often did, whether it was true that Sister Mary, along with the other nuns, had a shaved head. She quickly looked away in an attempt to purge herself of the thought. Sister Mary stood up.

'Let me ask you a question, Sissy. How would you like to go on a holiday?'

The thought of a holiday was so foreign to Sissy she couldn't make sense of what the Sister had asked her. 'A holiday?'

'Yes. Exactly. Each year the Diocese is contacted by our more fortunate Catholic families. Very generous families offering summer accommodation for those less fortunate living in the inner city. This year, for the first time, our parish has been chosen to nominate several children who we consider suitable. I have nominated you, Sissy.'

The Sister caressed the piece of paper she had been reading from.

'This letter is from a family who write that they are interested in taking a girl for the coming holidays. They have a daughter of their own who is about to turn twelve, your own age, as well as a younger son. I have spoken to your class teacher, Sister Anne, and she tells me that you have been a diligent and well-behaved student this year, with excellent examination results. I see this as your reward, Sissy.' Sister smiled. 'What do you think of the idea?'

Sissy wasn't sure what to think. She was reminded of Ruby Allison's story from earlier in the year. Perhaps she could return to the school in the new year with her own story of the ocean? A true story.

'Are you interested?' Sister Mary asked, when Sissy didn't reply.

'Yes ...' Sissy hesitated. 'I'll have to talk to my mother about this, Sister. She's never had me away.'

'Of course you would. And I will speak with her also. Your mother has always been a grateful woman. I'm sure she'll be happy for you.'

The Sister carefully folded the sheet of paper and returned it to the envelope.

'I want you to take this letter home to your mother. Is she able to read?' Sister frowned.

'Yes. She reads well.'

'Very well then. The details are contained in the letter. You must inform your mother that she will need to make her decision by the end of the week, as there are many girls in the school who would welcome such an opportunity.'

'Yes, Sister.'

Sister Mary took hold of Sissy's hand, a rare display of affection.

'This could be of great benefit to you, Sissy. Many of your people have never enjoyed such generosity.'

Your people? Sissy had no idea which people Sister Mary was referring to.

Sissy walked out into the street and found Betty doing handstands against the front wall of the House of Welcome, exposing her underwear.

'Betty, don't be doing that!' Sissy shouted. 'You'll be in trouble.'

'I don't care,' Betty said. 'I get in trouble anyway, for doing nothing at all.'

On the walk home Sissy showed Betty the letter and repeated what Sister Mary had said to her. If she expected Betty to be excited for her, Sissy was mistaken.

'I know why Sister Mary picked you,' Betty said, picking a stone up from the gutter and wrapping her fist around it.

'Why's that?' Sissy asked, so pleased with herself she began skipping along the street.

'It's because you have whiter skin than me. And your hair is nicer. Mine's like steel wool and yours is straw. You're exactly what them rich white people want, Sissy.'

Sissy stopped skipping, her cheeks flushed with anger. She stopped Betty from walking on.

'That's not true, and you know it. The reason I've been picked is because I did the best in class this year. Sister Mary said so. You remember the statue of Jesus Christ I won for getting the top mark for Catechism. The holiday has got nothing to do with my skin.'

'Makes no difference.' Betty smirked. 'It's why you get the best marks, too. White skin equals teacher's pet. That's the way it is. Always has been, and you know it.'

Sissy stamped the heel of her shoe against the bitumen.

'You can't believe that, Betty. I've never heard you talk like this before. You must be jealous.'

'I'm not jealous. I'm ...'

Betty aimed her stone at the street pole on the next corner. She pitched it. The stone skimmed through the air and slammed into the pole. She looked pleased with herself.

'Gee, I'd make a good hunter.'

'Not around here, unless you were after a stray cat, or a rat.'

Betty stopped at the corner and sat on the horse trough that hadn't been drunk from for decades. She had a deep frown on her face.

'What's wrong?' Sissy asked.

'I'm scared for you.'

Sissy sat next to her. 'Scared of what?'

'That maybe you won't come back.'

'Don't be silly. Of course I'll be coming back. It's only a holiday. For two weeks.'

'It doesn't matter what it is. One of my cousins, Valda, the Welfare told her mum, my auntie, the same story, that she was going on a holiday. Valda was excited, just like you are now. You know what happened to Valda? She disappeared.'

'I don't believe it. You're making this up, Betty, because you don't want me to go.'

'So what if I don't?' Betty shrugged. 'Even more than that I don't want you to disappear.'

Sissy stood up and tried skipping away, but couldn't recover her rhythm. She stopped, spread her legs apart, leaned forward and touched her forehead on the footpath, an exercise she'd learned in gymnastics class at school. No other girl had conquered the flexibility exercise. She looked through her legs at her upside-down friend.

'The story is not true and I won't be disappearing.'

'Please yourself,' Betty said. 'Don't blame me when they powder your face even whiter than it is and force you to church every day of the week.'

*

Three weeks later Sissy was seated on a wooden chair on her front verandah wearing her best dress, a daffodil print, and a matching yellow ribbon in her ponytail. A small suitcase sat at her feet. It contained another three dresses, a blue cardigan, a toilet bag and new pairs of socks and underwear. Sissy usually wore her mother's hand-me-down underpants several sizes too big. She was forever hitching them up as she ran around the schoolyard at lunchtime playing netball. As most other girls battled with the same predicament, the situation caused little embarrassment, except on the odd occasion when a pair of underpants fell around a girl's ankles. Sissy had made a visit to the Book Depot on Christmas Eve, where she swapped two paperback novels for four more plus the cost of a shilling. The books were also in the suitcase. She was a voracious reader and never left home without a novel in her schoolbag.

Sissy was admiring her dress when she heard the rusting hinges of a gate shriek further along the street. She looked up and saw Betty crossing the street towards her house. Betty stopped at the front gate, rested her chin on the edge of a splintered picket and looked down at the case.

'So, you're leaving for your holiday?'

'Yeah. The lady I'm staying with is coming soon to collect me. In her own car.'

Betty leaned a little too heavily on the gate. She hung on as it swung open.

'Your dress is so pretty, Sissy. I bet you must be happy that you're going away?'

In the weeks since Sissy had been offered the holiday by Sister Mary her enthusiasm for the holiday had gradually faded. She was no longer sure how she felt.

'I am happy. I was so excited last night,' she fibbed. 'I couldn't sleep properly with the nervous stomach ache I had.'

'So, you're really going then?'

'Of course I am.'

Betty hung her head over the fence and tucked her chin into her chest. Sissy heard her friend sob.

'You okay, Bet? What is it?'

Betty wouldn't answer. Sissy stood up and lifted Betty's chin. 'What's wrong with you, bub?'

Betty burst into tears. 'I'm sorry what I said about your skin and being teacher's pet. That was mean of me.'

Although what Betty had said had hurt Sissy's feelings, she'd been quick to let go of the pain. Her friendship with Betty meant the world to her.

'I don't care about any of that stuff. It doesn't matter to me. Honest.'

Betty jumped from the gate, lunged at Sissy and threw her arms around her.

'I'm going to be lonely without you for the rest of the holidays. Promise me that you'll come back.'

'Of course I'll be back. I cross my heart. Two weeks is fourteen days. I'll be home in no time.'

Betty wiped her face, stepped off the verandah, said goodbye in a rush and ran off down the street. Sissy was about to take her seat again when Betty popped up again at the open gate. She smiled, *all goofy-like*, Sissy thought. Betty walked over to her, leaned forward and shocked Sissy by kissing her on the lips.

'I love you, bub,' she said, before turning and running off a second time.

A few minutes later Sissy's mother, Miriam, came out of the house.

'Who was that just here talking to you?'

'Betty. She came to say goodbye.'

'She did? It's not like you're going on a world cruise or something. That kid's thick in the head. Like the rest of her mob.'

Sissy was quick to defend her friend. 'No, she's not, Mum. There's nothing wrong with Betty.'

'If that's the case, I'm raising a genius.'

Miriam lit a cigarette and sat on the verandah step, waiting for the stranger's car to arrive.

When Sissy had presented her mother with the letter of invitation from the church Miriam had not been as excited about the news as her daughter expected she would be. Nor did she try hiding her concerns about Sissy going off with a person neither of them had set eyes on.

'We don't know who these people are, Sissy. Or anything about them. Who are they?'

'Sister Mary knows them. She told me that the people who offer holidays are all good families.'

'But does she know them personally? What's written on a piece of paper doesn't mean a thing. One word is all you need to tell a lie.'

'Well, Sister Mary said she is going to come around and talk to you herself. They've had children for holidays before. If they were not good people then Sister Mary would know about it. There's nothing she doesn't know, Betty says.'

'Betty doesn't know a whole lot herself. If I ever come to rely on that kid for the safety of my own daughter I'll throw the towel in and let the Welfare take you off my hands.'

Miriam was even more nervous after reading the letter. She

twirled a length of Sissy's fringe around her finger and tucked it behind her daughter's ear.

'So you want to go off with this family?'

'Not if you don't want me to. I can stay here as well.'

Miriam had seen the excitement in Sissy's eyes and didn't want to disappoint her.

'You go, little Sis, and have a wonderful time.'

*

Tucked into the pocket of Sissy's floral dress was a telephone number and a sixpence coin that Miriam insisted her daughter take with her. Sissy was not to spend the money, under any circumstances, she had been told several times. Miriam explained that the coin was only to be used for an emergency. The telephone number was for Mrs Pellegrino, the Italian woman who ran the corner shop, who was happy to take messages for locals.

'I won't need the money,' Sissy said. 'I bet the family will have their own telephone. Sister Mary said that they are *well off.*'

A car turned into the street, a rare occurrence in the neighbourhood. A couple of boys who'd been playing with a rusting three-wheeler bike chased the car as it slowly moved down the road. Miriam dropped her cigarette and ground it under the heel of her shoe. The car stopped in front of their house, a powder blue sedan that shined like new. It was a small car, Sissy noticed, a two-door without a back seat. Few people on the street owned a car and Sissy had never ridden in one. She raised herself slightly out of her seat to catch a glimpse of the driver. The passenger side window was so clean and shining all she could see was her mother's apprehensive olive-skinned face reflected back to her.

The car door opened and a woman got out. Although it was a hot morning she wore a mauve-coloured woollen suit and a straw hat with matching mauve flowers sewn into the brim, shading her pale skin. She was *so* white Miriam was certain the lady was ill. The woman walked around to the front of the car but remained on the road. Miriam stepped onto the footpath and half curtsied before realising the stupidity of her action.

'I'm Miriam Hall, Sissy's mother.' She turned to the verandah.

'Sissy,' she called. Sissy refused to move from the chair. 'Come and say hello to Mrs ...'

The woman stepped forward and held out her hand. Miriam looked down at a set of manicured and polished fingernails.

'I am Mrs Coleman.' The woman spoke in a tone simultaneously husky and delicate, in a voice that appeared it might shatter at any moment. 'And this must be your daughter.'

Sissy stared at the sickly-looking woman standing in front of the car.

'Come here and say hello,' Miriam ordered her daughter.

Sissy stood up. 'Hello,' she coughed.

The pair of wayward kids on the trike circled the car several times before Miriam ordered them to get back to their own place. She did her best to be polite to her visitor, all the while resenting the self-conscious deference she displayed towards a person she did not know or care for. Sissy felt the shame of being both embarrassed of, and for, her mother.

After assuring Miriam that Sissy *will be taken wonderful care of*, Mrs Coleman opened the small boot at the rear of her car and stood back as Miriam loaded Sissy's case into the boot. Sissy could not take her eyes off the woman's face. Her skin was so transparent that lines of thin veins could be seen running down her cheekbones.

When it was time to say goodbye Miriam did so with as little display of emotion as was necessary. She nudged Sissy towards the open passenger door.

'Go on, bub. You be off.'

Sissy only relented and got into the car when Miriam stepped away from her daughter and retreated to the verandah.

'Go,' she said, with the wave of a hand. 'Off you go.'

It was only after she had buckled herself into the passenger seat and was driving away, seated next to the cold-looking woman in the funny hat, that Sissy grasped the reality of what she'd wished for so desperately weeks earlier. She turned her head and looked back at her mother, standing on the verandah with a hand to her mouth. The car turned the corner, out of the street, and stopped at a red light at the intersection. The corner was crowded with people, many of whom would never take a holiday to the coast, the mountains, or anywhere else. Some would never leave the suburb. Mrs Coleman leaned forward and peered out of the spotlessly clean front windscreen at the crowd. Sissy watched her face. The woman appeared to be in shock. She pushed the button down on the driver's side door, then turned to Sissy and ordered her to do the same.

'Lock your door, dear,' she said, her voice rising slightly.

Sissy turned to lock her own door and spotted Betty standing on the street corner, staring at her.

'Lock the door,' Mrs Coleman repeated, her voice crackling like a poorly tuned radio station.

As the light turned green Betty smiled at Sissy and shook her head up and down. The car lurched forward, braked suddenly and stalled. An elderly man had walked in front of the car. Sissy grabbed the doorhandle and jumped from the car before Mrs Coleman realised what was happening. Sissy bolted past Betty, screaming, 'Come on, you slow coach, come on.' Betty had always been the faster runner of the two girls. She drew alongside her friend within a block.

'Where we running to, bub?'

'I don't know,' Sissy gasped, 'I'm just running.'

'Come with me then, and hide.'

Betty took off and Sissy followed. They didn't stop running until they reached the local football ground several streets away. Sissy followed Betty behind the old grandstand at the far end of the oval. They crawled on their hands and knees into the darkness beneath. Betty climbed into the stand's wooden framework, followed by Sissy. They gathered their breath.

'You're going to be in such big trouble,' Betty said. 'Sister Mary will kill you.'

'She sure will. I don't care.'

'And your mum, she will probably kill you, too. After Sister Mary's finished with you.'

'No, she won't. My mum didn't want me to go on the holiday in the first place.'

'You sure of that? I thought you said she was happy for you to go?'

'She was only trying to be happy. It wasn't working. You know them worry lines she has above her eyes? Well, they were bulging out of her head today. I've never seen them worse. It was a sign.'

Betty grinned, as wide as a girl could.

'Well, even if Sister does kill you, I'll still be happy that you never went away in that car.'

'The car! Oh bugger,' Sissy said. 'My case is in the boot. I'll never get it back now.'

'Did it have anything good in it?'

'Yeah. My dresses and some books. And, hey! New undies and socks. I mean brand new underpants from the Junior Shop.'

'New undies!' Betty squealed. 'I wish I had a pair of new undies, instead of wearing my mum's bloomers.'

'Me too.' Sissy laughed. 'But it's too late now. And it doesn't matter.'

'Why's that?' Betty asked.

'Because I'm home, Betty. I'm home with you.'

'I knew you wouldn't go off with a strange lady.'

'No, you didn't.'

'I did so.'

Sissy climbed down, sat in the dirt and looked up at her friend.

'Tell me the truth. Did your cousin Valda really disappear when she went on a holiday?'

'Of course she did.' Betty jumped and landed next to Sissy. 'She disappeared for a week. She ran away and showed up back on my auntie's doorstep.'

'You never told me that part of the story.'

'No, I didn't. It was better to concentrate on the best part. That's how stories work.'

Barren Ground

Verity Borthwick

The wheel rumbled over a piece of road kill. Ruth glanced in the rear-view mirror, but all that remained was matted flesh and fur.

She angled the mirror to check on her husband. Slumped in the back seat, head lolling with the motion of the ute, his eyes half-closed, slitted in that way that made her feel he was watching her – even when he slept.

'You right back there?'

He grunted in reply. She changed gear, the clutch creaked.

She'd take the dam road – it was faster. But the first rains had already come; the monsoonal trough boiled up over the gulf and burst rain that fell in great sheets over the dry brush and made small, green things grow. What if the road was flooded?

Peter vomited. The acrid stench made her bile rise. He'd thrown up down the front of his shirt. She should stop. Clean him up. She'd done it before, more than once. But those were minutes they didn't have – she had hours to drive. She wound down the window and gulped fresh air.

The atmosphere was thick with humidity, that soupy feeling before a storm. The afternoon light had gone a strange, golden colour. Black clouds bunched on the horizon. Still far off, but she could see streaks of rain through the trees.

*

'Will you marry me, Ruthie?'

She would. What else was there to do?

His presence had always been too big. It filled the small town pub where he ordered a case and slung it back, one beer after another. His mates clustered around like flies on a dead horse, while she, she behind the counter pouring drinks, drunk field-hands swarming as the night grew long and guts filled with booze.

'Get on with it, girly, I'm thirsty as.'

How he'd stick his hand up her skirt when she was just fifteen.

'Seen your type,' hot breath scorching her ear, 'you girls, knowing beyond your years.'

Then he'd turn to her with that heart-stopping smile. Not many teeth that good in a town like hers. He was wiry muscle and tanned skin, tight jeans and a denim work shirt. He'd saunter in with a wink for her and the blood roared through her veins.

Those times he'd catch her on the way to the storeroom, and – when no one was watching – whisper she was the prettiest thing, she'd truly got at his heart. His mouth when he said the words. His mouth when he kissed her.

What hope did she have?

That handsome face weathering over the years. And her, what was left of her now?

He was a fire that burned her all up.

*

Her foot slackened. Pushing 130 but the needle began to drop.

The first spots of rain hit the windscreen.

She'd bandaged the wound. Start at the foot and work your way up, make it tight, not too tight or he'll lose the leg. Two black punctures oozing a little from the holes. Don't cut, don't suck, just bandage it and get the hell to hospital.

She could have radioed the flying doctors – they might've come.

She didn't.

*

'Barren cunt.'

'Don't you fucking touch me again, Pete, or I swear —'

'What, Ruth? What do you swear? Dying to hear it.'

'Can't talk to you when you're like this.'

'That's your excuse, that is.'

His ugly mouth scrunched, decaying teeth, the stench of rot. The grog had ruined him.

He was getting too close again. She put the table between them.

She had only to reach for a knife.

He flung open the kitchen door, went outside. She heard the axe, smack, it bit into bone. Smack. It severed. She knew it was her body he was butchering, not the cow's. Slicing muscle, sinew, bone. Separating limbs.

In her mind she threw boiling water over him, watched his skin begin to melt. She'd bludgeon him with the frying pan, push his carcass down one of the old mine shafts that dotted the hills like small, hungry mouths.

The way his eyes grew cold sometimes when he looked at her. She knew he was thinking of it. Caressing the idea like a new lover, getting a taste of it.

Only two of them out there. A hundred miles to the nearest neighbour.

The things isolation did to a person.

*

In the rain, the road became a red river. The tyres struggled, near bald, no money to go replacing them. The year had not been kind. Cows straggled through the brush like ghosts, grew thinner and thinner, and ribs and vertebrae rolled beneath the skin. Sometimes she saw them chewing the bones of their own dead, crunching them between flat teeth, trying to get at the sustenance.

The road kill grew bloated and wet, as though those mangled creatures might come alive again in the fog and drag their battered bodies from the bitumen.

Perhaps this year would be better – the rain had started early.

Perhaps the dam road would be closed.

Peter moaned. The windscreen wipers dragged across the glass, snagged in the muck of squashed insects and spattered mud. She imagined the blood in his veins growing thin like rainwater running down the windscreen. Inside him the venom pulsed towards his heart.

The tyres slipped. The ute slid.

*

Gone. Expelled from her body in a frightening rush of gore. Couldn't even catch it in her hands before it slipped into the toilet bowl. Sometimes these things just happen. No way to tell, but she wondered if it'd been a boy.

Peter reminded her of a wallaby she once hit, smacked into at ninety, tiny thing. Still alive when she got out to have a look. Small bundle of shivering fur and blood, eyes growing dull. She had stroked its soft ears, *I'm sorry, I'm so sorry.*

He walked through those days like a raw nerve, his body started to hunch, to curl in on itself, as though he forgot he once stood tall. His grief was a patch of fertile soil in an otherwise arid land. Soon small things began to grow. He let her stroke and comfort and confide. She had that power. He'd always been so hard before.

They sprung up like weeds in the garden. A tiny row of crosses you could see from the kitchen window. He always buried them himself. Even when there was no more than a handful of flesh.

*

She stood in the driving rain. The ute had slithered off the road into the soft, red soil. Peter's face through the rain-streaked window looked blurry, as though he'd started to disappear. She climbed in beside him, wiped up the mess on his face and shirt. He groaned and opened his eyes.

'Water.'

He drank noisily, like a child, and she fought to keep her expression calm, didn't want him to see her disgust.

He swallowed hard, cleared his throat. 'What's happening?'

'Ute's bogged.'

His eyes wide at that, dilated pupils so huge, black holes she could fall into and never find her way out. The whites of his eyes flecked with burst blood vessels that tangled like flooding creeks. His terror had a stink to it she could almost taste.

He clutched at the front of her shirt. 'Ruthie.'

Hadn't called her that in a long time. She shifted her weight away from him and her foot bumped against a shovel. Wrenching herself free, she grabbed it and got out.

The whole world was water. Rain hammered her body as she struggled to keep her footing, until she was soaked through and streaming with it. The shovel slipped from her hand. It lay at her feet, sinking a little in the mud. She stared at it, hand slowly clenching, unclenching, clenching.

Seconds passed.

Minutes.

She nudged the shovel with her foot as though it were a live thing.

The ute got bogged. Nothing I could do.

They'd believe her.

Finally, she bent down and picked up the shovel.

It bit deep in the dirt beneath the tyres. Mud, thick and iron red, bled back into the spaces she created. She gathered broken branches and jammed them into the gaps. She kicked over termite mounds and used the dry dirt to sop up some of the muck.

Turning the ignition, slowly with the clutch, slowly the accelerator. The ute writhed, wheels spinning. Then a catch, the wheels crushed the branches beneath them and the ute climbed back onto the road.

Ruth stopped and sat a while.

*

She pushed herself up in bed. He placed a tray on the counterpane. An eggcup, boiled egg with yolk that was dark yellow, fleshy. She thought she might retch. Peter had cut the toast into strips, the way his mother had done when he was feeling poorly.

'Brought you a cuppa too. Know you're feeling crook.'

'I don't want to do this.'

'What?'

'I'm not a person, Pete, just a body, a body for doctors to stick things into. For you to. I can't live like this.'

His lips were pressed together so hard they'd gone white. She hated how he looked in these moments. The ugly set of his mouth, the way his jaw trembled; a familiar grimace, the face of a man brought up to think tears were for sissies. She hated that she thought so too. He never cried in front of her. She only saw the aftermath, like picking your way through after the river spills its banks, and the ground is churned and open like a wound, the trees strewn this way and that, and splintered and half submerged in the mud.

'No more, Pete. It's done. I've started the pill. Can't go through it again. Can't.'

*

She could feel it up ahead, not too far, around the hill and down in the valley, the dam waiting, concrete, crouched. A monstrosity that carved its way through, eating the landscape and greedily stoppering the river for the better part of the year. But in the summer months, when the monsoon rolled over the state, and the creeks fed the streams, fed the rivers until it grew and grew and it was water roiling and branches breaking and clods of dirt falling from banks and houses slipping into the mire, it would overspill the dam wall, and pour over the road to seethe down the valley and rip up small trees and polish the rock and throw boulders along the bottom.

They turned the corner and the dam came into view. Her heart surged. Water everywhere. Pouring over the spillway, overflowing the road, tumbling down the valley and tearing at the banks.

She stopped the ute and stared. Tyres would labour in such a torrent, even good new ones. The ute would be carried away and both of them in it.

Peter began to convulse.

She opened the back door and slid in beside him. Drool streamed from the corner of his mouth. It was disappointing to see him like this. He was a strong man. A man who worked with his hands, who hammered and drilled and dominated. She had seen him wrestle a cow to the ground. She had seen him kill.

She stroked his head. I'm sorry, I'm so sorry.

*

'Oh my little Ruthie, how I love you so, 'specially your fingers, and all your little toes.'

He was singing that stupid song again. They were sitting in the old bathtub in the yard, and he was washing her back. Late summer, the last of the evening sun streaming through the eucalypts. Cicadas thrummed in the trees, the first evening mosquitoes droning around them. A few cows stood nearby, watching them with heavy-lidded eyes, mouths full of cuds, chewing, the occasional moan as a calf strayed too far.

'Oi, ya bunch of pervs. Quit making eyes at my wife.'

'They're just enjoying the last sun. Been a long day.'

'True, love, you're that dirty, think I'll be scrubbing all night. Always knew you was a dirty girl though, didn't I?'

She said nothing.

His fingers stole around her side and rested on her belly.

'You think it's a boy?'

She shrugged him off. 'How would I know, Pete? Right now it's a nothing. Hasn't even got fingers and toes.'

She hoped it was a boy. They had that in common.

'Maybe we could call him Frank, after me old pop.'

'Maybe.'

'You think I'll be a good dad, Ruthie?'

'Sure.'

'Build him a cubby, just like I had as a lad. Think he'd like that?'

'If you like.'

He put his arms around her body. An unexpected gesture, she wasn't sure what to make of it.

'Oi, now, don't come over here, you great sods. You've got your own trough.'

'That's it, Pete, I'm out.'

She leaped out of the bath, naked, dripping, as a cow pushed its head in and Peter yelled.

She couldn't help but smile.

*

The rain had slackened and the dam, visible once more, loomed above them. She could see the sign: Road closed ahead, do not attempt crossing. She could see the water running over the road.

They wouldn't question it if she did nothing.

Peter in the back.

His body breaking down. Blood running from his nose, she'd tried to stop it with a cloth, but it soaked through and still it flowed. He drifted in and out.

Couldn't really leave a person to die like that.

She edged the ute towards the crossing, keeping close to the dam wall, crawling in first gear. Water pushed back against the front tyres, a slight tug on the wheel, then the back wheels flooded and they were in the current. Water formed a bow wave at the front, splashing up over the windscreen, wipers back and forth, back and forth. Slowly – you know the drill, Ruthie – she crept forward, any sudden move, the tyres'd slip.

Peter was silent.

But she remembered his voice: 'Ease down on the clutch now Ruthie, shit, you've stalled again. No, no, don't worry, everyone does it when they're learning. We'll get her started again, no harm done. You've got this, love. Stay calm, you're doing great.'

Almost there, almost there, they hit a dip in the road. A horrible letting go and the ute was floating. It dragged sideways, towards the edge, towards the rocks and the river that churned beneath them.

She'd lost control.

She undid her seatbelt, started to wind down the window. Peter, how to get them both out, she couldn't.

It'd be beyond her.

She'd leave him.

A jolt, the ute bumped against the lip of the road, tyres on one side catching. She felt the rumble of gravel, of sediment, piled against the edge of the road. Grabbing the wheel, she slowly pressed her feet down, clutch, accelerator. The ute moved with her once more and they were on the other side.

*

He pushed her against the back wall of the pub, her skirt pulled up around her waist. The night was crackling with heat. Somewhere a fire was burning. She buried her face in his neck, his hair, breathed deep the scent of smoke. It was hot, too hot, and she was combusting.

A man staggered out of the pub and over to the bushes nearby. They froze, Pete's hand over her mouth. So still, but she could feel the pulse of him inside her. A crack of lightning illuminated them, and for a moment she was afraid someone might see. It went dark again. Her nostrils filled with the stink of old man's piss, and the drunk wove his way back and disappeared inside.

When Peter started thrusting again she thought she might scream.

*

At the last moment, as they neared the hospital – squatting at the edge of town with its rooms full of weeknight drunks and domestic assaults and limbs severed by heavy machinery – her foot had pressed down on the accelerator hard, so she almost sped right on past and on, on to the next town and the next.

But she braked, and parked, and watched as they wheeled away her husband. Somewhere back there they were injecting anti-venom into his body.

She looked down at her hands. They were red, red with iron mud and blood, Peter's blood. And in his leg those two black holes. One for each of them.

She sat in the waiting room, plastic chairs and polystyrene cups of machine coffee, dark smells disguised with bleach.

She waited.

At the far end of the hall, a door opened and a doctor walked the length of the hallway towards her. She tried to guess, but he was an upright man with an unreadable face, he delivered news like this every day, and still went home to cutlets and peas and mash with his family.

Outside an ambulance pulled up, its lights flashing red, blue, red, blue through the window.

'Mrs Walker?'

She stood so she could look him in the eyes. The lights from the ambulance lit his face so it appeared garish, carnival-like.

'My husband?'

Now his face rearranged and he spoke – the well-rehearsed platitude he recited night after night.

'There was nothing you could have done.'

He cleared his throat, a little uncomfortable now, the way she was staring at him.

'He was dead from the moment that snake bit him.'

Ruth sat back down in the chair. The ambulance lights went dark.

Miracles

Jennifer Mills

It was Deirdre Emerson's boy who was first affected. He went off to school at six and a half years old, ready for a day of alphabets and animals, and crept home a man of five feet ten, dressed like a fool in teenaged things from the lost property.

Deirdre said she very nearly closed the door in his face.

'Ma, it's me,' he said. 'Andy.'

She scrutinised his embarrassment. He was beginning to lose his hair.

'No, it's not,' she said. Her son reached out his arm, tugged up the too-short sleeve of a stranger's hoodie, and showed her the birthmark shaped like a whale on his right wrist. His skin was sweet and pale, she remembers, not quite as changed as the rest of him would indicate.

'What happened?' she asked.

But he would not talk about it, not then. He went into his room and stood there for a minute, looking at the teddy bears and the wooden trucks lined up along the sill, and then he began to pack them all away. Deirdre rang Jane Sweeney, the mother of a little girl named Elsa, a bright girl with a good ear for music with whom Andy had been accustomed to socialising. Jane was another single mother, a straight-talking woman and a great help whenever she felt she might go mad. She lived just down the road.

'Jane, Andy's come home all grown,' said Deirdre.

'It happens fast,' said Jane.

'Not this fast,' said Deirdre. 'He's about my age now.' She was only thirty-three. It had felt young the day before. Jane went quiet for a minute, then said she'd come right over. Deirdre stayed by the hall phone, listening out for movement upstairs.

'Elsa's home alone,' said Jane when Deirdre opened the door to her.

'It won't take long,' said Deirdre. 'You have to look at him.'

They found Andy sitting on the floor in the middle of his Lego and weeping silently. They watched him together.

'Shite,' said Jane. 'Are you sure it's him?'

'Hello, Mrs Sweeney,' said Andy, looking up at last. 'Where's Elsa?'

The two children had been in love in the pure way of the under sevens. Their mothers often made jokes about the wedding.

'She's safe at home,' said Jane Sweeney, beginning to doubt it. 'Are you all right? What happened?'

'I don't know,' said Andy. 'I can't remember.' His forehead gathered itself into a pained and grave expression that Deirdre Emerson knew well. She knelt on the floor, took his head into her arms and held it against her chest. Her breasts still hummed for this, but it was all wrong. She kissed the odd-smelling crown of his head. She hadn't even asked if he was okay.

'What are we to do,' she said, not expecting an answer. She stroked her son's hair, laying it flat behind his ear. There was a little grey coming through in places.

'I suppose you could try the doctor,' said Jane. 'I'm sorry. I've got to get back.'

*

The doctor gave Andy a thorough examination and pronounced him a perfectly healthy thirty-five-year-old male with exceptionally low blood cholesterol. Andy breathed into a contraption and was told his lungs were functioning at 110 per cent.

'There's nothing wrong with him at all,' marvelled the doctor. 'Quite the opposite.' Over the years the doctor had developed the kind of face that could be both stern and deeply humorous. She looked at Mrs Emerson until Mrs Emerson accepted the look and left the room. There was a rule about minors but the doctor felt it didn't apply.

The doctor rolled her chair over to sit beside Andy, close but not too close. 'Is there anything you want to tell me, Andrew? Anything at all you might feel ready to talk about? It can be just between us if you like.'

Andy shook his head. His long nose pointed at the floor between them as if it were too heavy for his face.

'What happened, Andy? How did it happen?' asked the doctor. There were clear regulations about making suggestions.

Andy looked up. Her eyes were too bright with the wonder of living. He shook his head. 'I honestly don't know,' he said. 'I don't remember anything before I got home.'

*

The rumours in the town ranged from time travel to alien abduction, but most reasonable people settled on a medical explanation. The doctor sent him to the hospital in the city for tests and observations, including at Deirdre's request a DNA comparison with his birth data, which the hospitals then kept on record. Since he was still technically six years old, Deirdre had no problem confirming that her son was indeed his own unique self without informing Andy she had enquired, but she felt awful about it and told him as soon as she got the results.

'It's okay, Ma,' he said. 'You can't be too careful. I would have done the same.'

Who was this grown man with a formed and empathetic character? He was washing the dishes without being asked. She'd been cheated of creating him, and yet there was so much to be proud of. He had a fine posture, a calm voice, he wasn't panicking. Apart from the crying jag among the Lego just that once, she hadn't seen him suffering from his situation.

'They asked if they could study you,' she said. She put a hand to his shoulder. The new T-shirt she'd bought him was a dull grey-green that seemed to suit his subdued personality. Her boy had always been a little sensitive. He thought for a while before he turned.

'I just want to get on with things, Ma,' he said. 'Put it behind me.'

He was qualified for nothing but neither was he lacking in intelligence; wherever he had been, he seemed to have been educated well (and, Deirdre could not help but notice, very cheaply). Once he was cleared of known contagions, Howard found him a position in the council office, where he registered dogs and photocopied planning applications. It was entry level but there was room for advancement and Andy spent most of his time behind the scenes so did not have to see the people craning for a look at him through the inky glass. There was nothing much for them to crane at. He was handsome enough for his mother and orderly about his work and made no trouble in the council or the town. If anything he was a little boring, a man of few words and fewer stories.

For a while things returned to normal. Andy became a regular citizen. The legal centre helped him to apply to have his birth certificate backdated so that he could vote and drive, which he did well enough; so whenever Officer McKinley pulled him over he knew it was just to get a closer look at him. He was good to his mother, helped around the house and did the shopping, volunteered once a fortnight for Meals on Wheels, and seemed to be ageing now at a regular pace. There was nothing much else you could say about it apart from that it was strange.

About seven months after Andy had surprised her, Deirdre Emerson opened the door to another apparent stranger. This one was a younger man, perhaps in his late twenties, and she put her hand to her chest as in a mild panic of nerves he introduced himself as Harry Sifton. The paper boy. Just that morning she had waved to his retreating eleven-year-old figure as he rode off down the street, straw hair sticking unruly from beneath his baseball cap.

'Can I talk to Andy?' he asked. He held the baseball cap in one hand and ran the other through his hair, which he still wore long, although it had browned a bit. His hands were large and his voice had developed a lovely baritone.

'Of course.' She let him in and called Andy into the kitchen. The two men declined her offer of tea, and soon retreated into Andy's room where they talked for over an hour. She peeled the potatoes very quietly, but the one time Deirdre heard their voices raised it was in laughter.

After Harry Sifton had refused dinner three times, shaken her hand, embraced Andy and gone home to tell his parents, they sat down over a simple meal of lamb chops, broccoli and mashed potato.

'Well?' she asked Andy.

'He doesn't remember anything either,' said Andy. She watched him eating, slow and focused, but his skin, flushed from the excitement, emphasised the boy's features hidden beneath the man's. She wondered if she'd ever stop seeing them.

'You used to hate broccoli,' she said.

He squinted at her for a second. 'I remember,' he said. 'You told me it was tiny trees they'd cut down on a miniature planet. Gone to all that trouble just for me.' He used his knife and fork in the emphatic way his father used to have. He was four years older now than Jeff had been when she'd last seen him.

'I stole the idea from *The Little Prince*,' she said. Her fingers made the shape of the tiny chainsaw but she didn't make the sound. 'You always fell asleep before the chapter was over.' There was a heaviness in her throat. She had learned to think of it as gaining a brother, but the appearance of Harry Sifton, and then the effort of imagining Mary Sifton's face, reminded her of what had been taken away. All that time they might have spent together, all that growing. And yet it was hard, with his healthful figure across the table, to justify bad feelings.

'Could it have been, perhaps,' she asked, 'another planet?'

In the distance she could hear Elsa practising on the piano Jane had bought her. The girl had a wonderful ability, and time to build upon it.

'It could be anything, Ma,' said Andy. 'I really don't remember. I'm sorry.'

'Don't you apologise to me,' she said, 'you've done nothing wrong.' Surprised by the anger in her voice, she swallowed down a whole glass of water. He laid his knife and fork neatly on the empty plate and waited for her to finish her meal before he cleared the table.

*

Andy had been treated as an anomaly, but after word got around about Harry Sifton, some families with young children began to leave the town. The wealthier ones went first, their principles about the public school unravelling behind them like a cotton thread caught on a nail. Deirdre and Jane sat together in the park, friends again after a brief but necessary conflict. They were watching Andy pushing Elsa on the swings, his long arms strong in the sunlight. Deirdre herself felt indescribably heavy in comparison.

'I suppose you could send her to her father's,' said Deirdre.

'Not on your life,' said Jane. 'And anyway, there's the piano now.'

Andy glanced at his watch between pushes. Andy and Harry Sifton had started going round together, and it was wonderful for Deirdre to see Andy with a friend again, even if it meant he was off drinking. Most of his old playmates were still in Yvonne Yang's first-grade class and he would sometimes watch them wistfully from outside the fence as they ran across the playground at lunchtime. Only Elsa had not faltered in her friendship. If anything, her adoration of Andy had intensified. It was almost concerning, though it didn't seem to concern Jane.

'You know I lost one before,' said Deirdre. 'Years ago.' Her voice was very quiet.

'You never told me that,' said Jane.

'She was twelve weeks premature. Hardly took a breath.' Deirdre took a deep one now.

Jane sat back and put her hands against her sides. 'I'm so sorry, Deirdre,' she said.

Deirdre waved at her face, dismissing its shown feelings as a weakness. 'Years ago,' she said.

'Higher, higher,' squealed Elsa. The muscles under Andy's birthmark flexed.

'Whichever way you look at it, they're miracles,' said Jane.

'He always felt that way,' said Deirdre.

*

The Hartley girl was gone for twenty-four hours. Never turned up at the school, didn't come home, a search out all night, police, everything. They were lining up the bus drivers for interviews when she showed up at her house for breakfast, apparently unharmed, and nicely fitted out in a tweed skirt, cream cotton blouse and sensible shoes. Nobody knew where she had got these items. The shoes were well worn in.

'Don't worry,' she told her parents. 'I feel absolutely fine.'

She found work in the library. When anyone asked her about it, her smile was a little watered down, perhaps, but it was still there, bright enough. It was Phoebe Hartley who began to use the word 'taken' to describe her situation, to excuse her absence from history and her lack of paperwork. The others picked it up from her. Deirdre didn't like it. But Phoebe Hartley was such a positive girl, it would have been cruel to test her optimistic nature with too many questions, just as it was hard to stop thinking of her as a girl, even now that she was nearly forty.

After the Hartley girl, there was little Suzie from the Chinese restaurant who was only three before she was nineteen overnight. Suzie made a pretty waitress, and was so calm and at peace with her transformation that half the town developed unexpected cravings for gong bao chicken and the little pancakes Mrs Chu served sliced into segments and hot enough to burn your mouth. Harry, who had kept his paper route, soon started carrying flowers on his bicycle, courting her, and her parents somehow accepted this, even grew quickly fond of him, because the two of them seemed to fit together so easily; it was as though they already shared a history. He learned to say hello and ask after the health of Suzie's grandmother in terribly accented Cantonese. Suzie's parents had been slow to start a family, and each of them had sometimes privately regretted their delay. The business had needed a great deal of their attention. But now the prospect of early grandchildren seemed like justice.

All the children who were affected had the same calm, the same ability to reassure. And after half-a-dozen had been returned, their blood tests and examinations revealing an unblemished wellbeing, a clean slip through time, everybody became used to them. They were well-adjusted, happy people, kind to us all, ready to make a contribution. It was very doubtful that our own hands would have moulded them into better people. Surely they could be no more readied for the world of responsibilities into which they were suddenly thrust? Indeed the results were so impressive that some new families began to move into the district, particularly those with multiple school-aged children. They didn't announce why they'd come but if you took them aside they would often admit that a third pair of hands at home, a third income, could really make a difference.

'If only you'd be taken,' exhausted parents would tell their screaming two-year-olds, only half in jest. Deirdre overheard them in the park and found it upsetting, but she would never be the one to make a fuss.

*

It was her father in America who gave Elsa the bracelet for her birthday, but Andy who was there to buckle it to her wrist. It was pink and it had a little chip in it that Jane could follow along on her phone. Elsa loved it so much that Andy considered selling them out of the garage on Saturday mornings, to make a little extra money. He was putting aside a deposit for a place of his own.

'I want to be grown up,' Elsa told him, her face too close and fresh-smelling, 'so I can come and live with you at your house.'

Jane rolled her eyes. To Deirdre it seemed abominable to tag and track her like some animal, but she would have done the same if it had been available for Andy, if she had known. The bracelets were new inventions, still a prototype, apparently. Everyone marvelled over it at the party.

'Now we'll know where you are, even if you're taken,' said Andy. Deirdre still flinched at the term.

'You all say you don't remember anything,' she said. 'So how —'

'We don't,' said Phoebe, the ripple in her smile like a sail catching a sweet breeze.

Deirdre opened her mouth to speak, but Andy's hand was raised.

'I can't have this conversation again,' Andy said. When he was cross with her he looked just like his father.

'The important thing is that you're alive,' she said, remembering to list her miracles.

He was picking up his car keys. 'I'm going to get a drink, if anyone's interested.' Harry sprung up, the two of them closing ranks. An arm against a shoulder on the way out the door, the solidity of men.

Go on and leave me, Deirdre thought, but watched his car back out in silence. She felt sixty years old.

She and Jane started packing up the princess toys and sheet music and adult outfits Elsa had been given in case she suddenly grew into them. Elsa herself was asleep. The party had been exhausting, now that there were all these strangers to get used to. Some of them played with the children and some of them drank out on the terrace with the parents and some of them stood around like people do at parties, afraid of mistaking their place, but in a good-natured and patient way. None of them remembered anything, and people kept repeating – even Deirdre said it – the important thing was that they were alive and well, the important thing was surviving. She picked up the cardboard box the wristwatch had come in, and wondered if it would make any difference.

'Have you thought about having another one?' Jane whispered.

'I couldn't take it,' said Deirdre, crushing the small box flat.

Jane would sometimes run across to their place on a sunny afternoon if there was a program on the television Deirdre or Andy might be interested in watching, or if she had made too many honeyjoys, so Deirdre didn't worry until she saw her friend was waving her phone in the air. Elsa had been napping but was now not in her room. The three of them gathered around the screen to watch as a little green dot moved slowly across it, pulsing slightly, before stopping in the park.

It was five blocks, but they got in Andy's car and he drove them there, Jane white as a sheet in the back, Deirdre out of words. Andy leapt out first and ran. Elsa was sitting in the grass looking at the sky. She acted as though she couldn't see them. She was still just seven years old.

'I think I sleepwalked,' said Elsa, in a muffled voice.

'You're all right, you're all right,' said Jane, releasing her.

'Come on,' said Andy. 'Let's get her home.'

Deirdre found that she was shaking.

This situation repeated itself several times over the following weeks, with Elsa found in different locations: a roundabout, the playground, once beneath the birdbath in a neighbour's back yard. Andy blamed the stress.

One day the three of them got out of the car on the corner where the dot had stopped, expecting Elsa, and found instead a pink bracelet hanging from a stumpy branch of a pine tree, rocking slightly in the wind.

*

Well, she always had that wonderful ear for music. And really, it was a gift, that kind of memory. It would have been, in other circumstances, something magical. But you know her mother taught her to be forward, and they say the character is formed very early in life, that even the best teachers can't do much with them after a certain age. In her fifties, she has just the same insistent confidence she's always had. Life, we tried to tell her, was never meant to be fair.

We can't blame Jane, but we can't help thinking it would have been better if Elsa had learned to keep things to herself. If the children had gone on saying they were taken, if they had never been reminded of the things that were done to them, their hands would have stayed steady, their work conscientious, their voices kind and calm and reassuring. Oh, maybe there were always consequences lurking in them, unseen injuries that rippled slowly outwards and would eventually spill into the world, but maybe there were not. Maybe we could have stayed just proud, and not have had to hate ourselves for what we had allowed to happen. It was after Elsa that it all came apart, and for that we can't forgive her.

Trampoline

Joe Rubbo

When we get home from school my brother's dad, Jerry, is out the front, leaning against a truck that has a trampoline strapped to the back of it. He's holding a cigarette between thumb and forefinger, the burning tip disappearing into his cupped hand. As we pull into the driveway, he takes one last drag, drops the butt to the road, and crushes it with the heel of his boot. There are two guys I've never seen before sitting on the nature strip, one of them chugging down a carton of iced coffee.

Mum yanks up the parking brake and we all sit there listening to the engine tick over. No one says anything. The car is starting to heat up now the air conditioning's shut off. I can feel my thighs suctioning to the seat. Mum billows her shirt with pinched fingers and blows the hair off her face. After a while she says to my brother, 'Do you know what your dad's doing here?'

Justin picks at the vinyl flaking away on the doorhandle.

'Nup.'

'He's giving you a trampoline, by the looks of it,' Mum says, taking the keys out of the ignition and holding them in her fist.

Jerry is still standing over by the truck, his head cocked to one side like he can't work out what the problem is. His face is scrunched up hard against the sun. I wave at him, but I don't think he sees me because he doesn't wave back.

'You know about this?' Mum says.

Justin looks at her, tongue wiggling the silver stud below his lip. 'Nup.'

'Bullshit, Justin. You could've given me some warning.'

'I didn't know about it. I don't even want a trampoline.'

'I do,' I say, sticking my head between their seats. 'I want a trampoline.'

They both ignore me.

'Jesus, I'm starting to cook in here,' Mum says, cracking the door. 'You better go and say hello.'

Justin gets out of the car and walks over to Jerry, his thumbs hooked underneath his backpack straps. Jerry punches him in the arm and Justin shrugs away. They both stand there looking at each other. The two men I don't know get up off the nature strip and brush the dry grass from their jeans.

Me and Mum go round the back of the car and she pops the boot, which lets out a fart of banana-scented heat. She gives me a couple bags of shopping and takes all the others herself.

'Jerry,' she yells, slamming the boot shut with her elbow. 'Don't even think about it.'

Jerry just waves back at her, smiling.

'And pick up your bloody cigarette butt.'

I follow Mum through the front gate.

'If he wants to put it in the backyard,' I say, 'then you should let him.'

'Is that right?' she says, kicking the gate shut behind me.

Nintendo is crouched behind his kennel, strings of saliva hanging from his mouth. When we get close he darts out and starts running rings around Mum, his nails scraping against the brickwork. Mum pushes him away with the toe of her shoe. He comes at me next and I swing the shopping bags until one of them, heavy with tins of baked beans, hits him in his side. He yelps and scuttles off back behind his kennel.

'Bloody Jerry,' Mum says, opening the front door.

'He's all right.'

'What would you know about it?'

We go inside and I kick off my shoes so I can feel the slate tiles, cool against my feet.

'He can do a Rubik's Cube without looking it up on YouTube,' I say.

Mum laughs. 'That's because he doesn't have a job.'

'He brought us a trampoline. That's good.'

'Good example of him being a dickhead, more like.'

We dump the shopping on the bench and Mum starts going through the bags, looking for the Viennetta. She pulls it out of a bag and pushes it sideways into the freezer and then starts putting away the rest of the shopping. I get myself a juice box from the fridge and punch in the straw.

'That bloody game,' she says, head in the pantry. 'Now this.'

She's talking about the arcade machine, Jerry's last present for Justin. It's one of those real old ones – takes up nearly a quarter of Justin's room and it only has *Space Invaders* on it. He still makes me pay twenty cents every time I want to play.

'Jerry likes big presents.'

'Jerry likes to be an inconvenience.'

'Why's that?'

'Shit, I don't know. Can you see if the dog's got water?'

'Yep.'

But instead I go into my dad's study and pull up the blinds so I can see what's going on out in the street. They've untied all the ropes holding the trampoline in place. Jerry is standing up on the truck, while the other guys are down on the street. They lower it down slowly. Jerry's face is deep red, the veins in his neck bulging blue, and I can see the sweat pouring off him from here. The other guys don't seem all that bothered. Justin's sitting on the kerb, both thumbs poking his mobile phone.

Once they've got the trampoline on the road, Jerry stands there with his hands on his waist, breathing hard. Then, when Jerry's ready, they hoist the trampoline up off the road and shuffle over towards the house. I can hear Jerry swearing from here.

I go back into the kitchen and wait for them to come around the side, standing by the window and sucking at my juice box until I hit air.

'Did you water the dog?' Mum asks.

Nintendo is cutting sick, running in circles and nipping at the men as they walk across the garden.

'Robyn,' Jerry yells, loud enough for us to hear him through the glass. 'Do something about this dog, would you?'

Mum doesn't look up from chopping carrots. 'We need to get a bigger dog,' she says, not really to me. 'One that bites more than just feet and ankles.'

'Like a German shepherd?'

Mum gives me the look that tells me it's time to stop talking.

They put the trampoline in the corner of the backyard, right next to the fat palm tree. Jerry shakes hands with one of the men and then they slouch towards the driveway. I can hear the truck grinding through the gears as they drive off. The trampoline covers most of the lawn.

Jerry comes over and opens the kitchen door. He only sticks his head in.

'So,' he says, 'how about that?'

Mum keeps chopping, her knife thudding harder and harder into the board.

'Pretty rad,' I say.

'I guess you're not happy about it.'

'Fuck off, Jerry.'

'Fair enough.'

Justin comes in, drops himself onto the couch, and turns on the TV. Bear Grylls is on the screen, shirtless and shivering by a lake. His lips are bright blue and he's talking at the camera about the importance of keeping warm.

'Is that it?' Mum says to Jerry.

'Unless you're going to invite me to stay for dinner.'

'Ha!'

'Just,' Jerry says, 'aren't you going to give her a bounce?'

'Maybe later.'

'I will,' I say.

Jerry winks at me. 'Well, I better head off.'

'Bye, Jerry,' I say.

Mum and Justin don't say anything.

'Justin, I'm gonna get going.'

'Yeah, bye, Dad.'

Jerry hangs there a little longer, looking at Justin. He taps the doorhandle with the heel of his palm and says, 'Okay.'

He closes the door and walks back around the side, all the time looking at the trampoline like he built it or something. Mum doesn't watch him go. She gathers up most of the sticks of celery, carrot and cucumber and puts them into Tupperware containers. The rest she puts on a plate, which she slides over the kitchen bench towards me.

'Eat these. Now.'

I climb up onto the stool, pick up a celery stick, and watch Mum as she scoops up the bright curls of vegetable peel from the bench and dumps them into the bin. She stops by the sink and looks at the trampoline, its shadow sliding across the lawn.

'Fucking cunt,' she says.

'I heard that,' Justin says.

'Is there any peanut butter?' I say, holding up the finger of celery.

*

Me and Mum have a bet going. See how long it takes Dad to notice the trampoline. I say next week. She says never. But he surprises us both by noticing it that night over dinner. I guess it is almost the only thing you can see when you look out the glass doors next to the dining table.

'Pretty big,' he says, folding the newspaper and tucking it under his elbow.

'Yep,' Mum says.

'You boys must be happy.'

I nod. Justin doesn't look up from his plate.

'Didn't he get you that thingo once?' Dad says, pointing his fork at Justin.

'*Space Invaders* machine,' I say.

'Yeah,' Dad says.

'Yeah,' Justin says.

Dad laughs. 'What's Jerry doing, looting theme parks or something?'

'I don't see why he can't just give me cash,' Justin says.

'Hear, hear,' Mum says.

'Cash is the last thing you'll ever get from Jerry,' Dad says.

Mum cuts him a look. 'Not now.'

'Did Jerry tell you how the dogs are going?' Dad asks.

'Leave him alone,' Mum says, forking some salad into her mouth and looking at Justin.

But Dad has to retell the story about Jerry and his venture into greyhound racing, even though we've all heard it a million times. There's no stopping him now that he's gotten started. It's his favourite Jerry story at the moment.

A few months ago, Jerry showed up with a racing dog he called Mixed Harmony. He used to keep her at a kennel near Kinglake. On Black Saturday, Jerry and his friends drove out to see how Mixed Harmony was coming along, somehow clueless to the fact there was a pretty serious bushfire shaping up. By the time they got to the kennels it was starting to get scary and the trainer had already started herding all the dogs onto a truck.

He was furious when he saw Jerry and his mates pull up, told them to get lost. They'd driven over two hours in the scorching heat just to see her. But Jerry didn't mind. In that short time, he'd already gotten all he wanted out of the trip. As the dogs were moving across the yard, something seemed to startle them and they started running towards the truck, their long bodies low to the ground as they picked up speed. Jerry had stood by the car a moment, hills burning around him, and watched Mixed Harmony kick out wide of the pack. She'd started near the back, but made up ground quick. The way Jerry described it, the whole world seemed to slow down except for Mixed Harmony. 'First up the ramp,' he told us, excited. 'And that's against some real champions.'

But Mixed Harmony never even made it onto the track. She was too skittish. Jerry felt obliged to take her on as a pet. He calls her Harm for short.

'You couldn't invent it,' Dad says.

'Yeah, yeah,' Mum says. 'Laugh it up.'

'He told me he's met someone,' Justin says, squashing peas with the back of his fork. 'Reckons he's in love.'

Mum snorts. 'Yeah, right.'

'He's moving to Broome to be with her, says she's going to get him a job on a pearl farm.'

Mum puts down her knife and fork. The sounds of cicadas fill up the silence.

'Well,' Dad says after a while, 'good for Jerry. I'm sure Harm will appreciate the warmer weather. Always cold, greyhounds.'

After the plates are cleared, Mum brings out the Viennetta

and puts it in front of Justin. There are fourteen candles sticking out of it.

'You forgot one,' I say.

Mum crosses her arms. 'They come in packs of seven.'

'Don't you dare sing,' Justin says.

Dad looks at Justin. 'Is it your birthday, mate?'

*

After dinner I go out to the trampoline. It isn't like my friend Ben Keenan's – those ones with the tightly woven black material that don't give up much bounce. This one is bigger by half. The bed is blue and there's a faded red cross in the middle. The springs are fatter than my forearms. I clamber up and the cross-hatched material pinches at my bare feet.

The trampoline sends me up high and straight. In the air, it's like I've got a couple of minutes to do whatever the hell I want. I run through all the tricks I know. Bum, back and belly drops. Front flips. Backflips. Three-eighties, arms helicoptering around me.

At my highest I can see all the tennis balls stuck on our roof, my head almost touching the palm fronds. Nintendo watches me the whole time from behind the paperbark tree, ears flat, tongue hanging out.

After a while the Viennetta feels like it might come out of me so I stop bouncing and sit down. The trampoline cradles my bum. The sun drops behind the next-door neighbour's prickly pears and the garden turns a dark green.

I lie back and look up. The blue in the sky is giving way to black. Stars are starting to punch through. It's then, running my hand over the trampoline, that I feel it. A rough patch.

I kneel close to inspect it. One of the threads has come loose. There's a hole in the very centre of the cross. But then, the hole isn't very big at all. I can just wiggle two fingers through to the other side.

Dreamers

Melissa Lucashenko

'Gimme an axe.'

The woman blurted this order across the formica counter.
When the shopkeeper turned and saw her brimming eyes he
took a hasty step backward. His rancid half-smile, insincere to
begin with, vanished into the gloomy corners of the store. It was
still very early. Outside, tucked beneath a ragged hibiscus bush,
a hen cawed a single doubtful note. Inside was nothing but this
black girl and her highly irregular demand.

The woman's voice rose an octave.

'Give us a Kelly, Mister, quick. I got the fiver.'

She rubbed a grubby brown forearm across her wet eyes.
Dollars right there in her hand, and still the man stood, steepling
his fingers in front of his chest.

It was 1969. Two years earlier there had been a referendum.
Vote Yes for Aborigines. Now nobody could stop blacks going
where they liked. But this just waltzing in like she owned the
place, mind you. No *please*, no *could* I. And an axe was a man's
business. Nothing good could come of any Abo girl holding
an axe.

The woman ignored the wetness rolling down her cheeks. She
laid her notes on the counter, smoothed them out. Nothing
wrong with them dollars. Nothin at all. She pressed her palms
hard onto the bench.

'Are. You. Deaf?'

'Ah. Thing is. Can't put my hand to one just at the ah. But why not ah come back later, ah. Once you've had a chance to ah.'

The woman snorted. She had had fifty-one years of coming back later. She pointed through an open doorway to the dozen shining axes tilted against the back wall. On its way to illuminate these gleaming weapons, her index finger silently cursed the man, his formica counter, his cawing hen, his come back later, his ah, his doorway, and every Dugai who had ever stood where she stood, ignorant of the jostling bones beneath their feet.

Her infuriated hiss sent him reeling.

'Sell me one of them good Kellys, or truesgod Mister I dunno what I'll do.'

*

As twenty-year-old Jean got off the bus, she rehearsed her lines.

'I'm strong as strong. Do a man's eight hours in the paddock if need be. Giss a chance, missus.'

When Jean reached the dusty front yard of the farm on Crabbes Creek Road, and saw the swell of May's stomach, hard and round as a melon beneath her faded cotton dress, she knew that she couldn't work here. When May straightened, smiling, from the wash basket, though, and mumbled through the wooden pegs held in her teeth Jean? Oh thank God you're here, she thought that perhaps she could.

Ted inched up the driveway that afternoon in a heaving Holden sedan. Shy and gaunt, he was as reluctant to meet Jean's eye as she was to meet his. This white man would not be turning her doorhandle at midnight. She decided to stay for a bit. If the baby came out a girl she would just keep going, and anyway, maybe it would be a boy.

The wireless in the kitchen said the Japanese were on the back foot in New Guinea but from Crabbes Creek the war seemed unlikely and very far away. What was real was endless green paddocks stretching to where the scrub began, and after that the ridge of the Border Range, soaring to cleave the Western sky. The hundred-year-old ghost gums along the creek; the lowing of the cows at dawn: these things were real. A tame grey lizard came to breakfast on the verandah, and occasionally Jean would glimpse the wedgetails wheeling far above the mountain, tiny smudges halfway to the sun. May had seen both eagles on the road once, after a loose heifer had got itself killed by the milk truck. You couldn't fathom the hugeness of them, and the magnificent curve of their talons, lancing into the unfortunate Hereford's flank.

Jean fell into a routine of cleaning, cooking, helping May in the garden, and sitting by the wireless at night until Ted began to snore or May said ah well. Of a morning, as she stoked the fire and then went out with an icy steel bucket to milk the bellowing Queenie, Jean would hear May retching and spewing in the thunderbox. One day, two months after she first arrived, there was blood on the marital sheets. Jean stripped the bed, and ordered May to lie back down on clean linen. Then she took Ted's gun off the wall and shot a young roo from the mob which considered the golden creek flats their own particular kingdom. A life to save another life. Jean made broth from the roo tail. And you can just lie there till it's your time, she said crisply. It's not like I can't manage that little patch of weedy nothing you like to call a garden.

The life inside May fought hard to hang on. Her vomiting eased, and as the weeks passed the terror slowly left her face. When her time drew very near, an obvious question occurred to May. Didn't Jean want children of her own? A husband?

Not really, said Jean, and who would I marry anyway, and is that Ted home already.

May ignored the possibility of Ted. The war will be over soon, there'll be lots of blokes running about the place. You said you like babies.

Yes, Jean said, expressionless. Other people's babies. Now lie flat, or I'll never hear the end of it from Himself.

You mean from you, laughed May, for the doctor had said the danger was past. Baby kicked happily now whenever it heard Ted's voice coming up the stairs.

The next week, Ted drove his wife into Murwillumbah at speed, churning dust and scaring fowl all the way to the hospital. They returned three days later with a squalling bundle on the back seat. Jean held her breath, waiting to discover if she could stay.

We called him Eric, Ted told the water tank proudly. After me old dad.

Eric, repeated Jean, reaching down to stroke a tiny pink cheek.

Later May reported the doctor's verdict: make the most of this one, because there would be no more babies for her.

*

Eric was a plump laughing baby, and then an adored toddler, always wandering, always in the pots and pans.

Come to Jean-Jean, she would cry, and Eric would ball his little fists and hurtle joyfully into her, clutching at her shins. She lifted him high in the air, both of them squealing with delight, until May came out laughing too, and demanded her turn. If the child cried in the night, it didn't matter to him who arrived to comfort him. Eric was at home in the world, because the world had shown him only love and tenderness.

'If it wasn't for the fact that I feed him,' May said casually, tucking herself back into her blouse one day, 'I don't think he'd know that I'm his mother, and not you.'

'Oh, he does!' protested Jean, feeling a sudden thread of fear unspooling in her gut. 'And he's the spit of you, anyway. What would he want with a mother like me?' May glanced at Jean's brown face, her black eyes and matchstick limbs.

'You're not all that dark. You're more like Gina Lollobrigida,' she said generously. 'Exotic. Plenty of men would want you for a wife.'

'But would I want them?' Jean retorted, a question that had never occurred to May.

After that, Jean held the boy a little less when his mother was around. She let May go to him at night, and was careful to be outside more often helping Ted in the paddock when Eric needed his afternoon bath. May thought they were pals, but Jean knew she could be flung away from the farm with one brief word, catapulted back to the Mission, even, if she couldn't scrape a better life up out of her own effort and wits.

*

May confessed tearfully one day that she had briefly allowed Eric – now struggling on her lap to regain his lost freedom – to stray into the Big Paddock. 'I actually felt my heart stop. I never knew you could love anyone so much.'

But I did, thought Jean, with a pang so fierce it made her gasp.

'He's a terror for wandering, all right. Pity we can't bell him like Queenie,' was what she finally managed.

May caught the bus to town and returned with a tinkling ribbon that had had six tiny silver bells sewn onto it by kind Mrs O'Connell. With the ribbon pinned between his shoulderblades, Eric could be heard all over the house and yard, a blue cattle bitch lurking by his side as constant as a shadow.

The second time Eric got himself lost, he was gone half an hour. They finally found him playing in the mud on the far side of the duck house, three strides from the dam, the ribbon torn off by the wire around the vegie patch. The women, who had each thought that the other was watching Eric, quietly resolved to say nothing to Ted. That night Jean woke the household screaming that a black snake had got in and bitten the baby – but it was only a bad dream.

It was the barking that alerted them to Eric's third disappearance, a few weeks later. Peeling spuds on the verandah, Jean became aware of the dog's frenzied yelps, and realised that she hadn't heard Eric's bell for a minute or more. She rocketed to her feet, sending spuds all over the silky-oak floorboards, and ran blindly to the yard where the dog was circling in agitation.

Jean and May circumnavigated the house, then the paddocks, with no result. Eric would not be found. A search party fanned out, desperate for clues. Here the boy had scratched at the damp creek bank with a twig from the largest gum. Here he had uprooted one of Queenie's dry pats, to discover what crawling treasures lay beneath. But the signs petered out where the pasture of the Big Paddock turned into scrubby foothills, and nothing was revealed – not that day, nor the next, nor in the awful weeks that followed – that could bring Eric back to them. The boy had quite simply vanished.

*

Nobody could fathom why Ted and May kept the dark girl on. But who else would understand why Ted could never go straight to the Big Paddock in the mornings anymore, and took the long way past the dam instead? Who else shared May's memory of Eric tilting his head to eat his porridge? The high tinkling bell-note of a king parrot's call made Jean catch May's eye, and neither of them had to say a word. And so the terrible thing which would have driven any other three people far apart instead bound them together.

In spring, Ted planted a silky oak sapling between the house and the gate. At its foot lay an engraved granite boulder. May took to sitting beside Eric's rock at odd hours of the day and night, gazing past the ghost gums, searching the distant hills. When the wet season arrived they sat, waiting to see what would wash down to them from the forested gullies. But the foaming brown floodwaters of the creek revealed as little as the search parties had. Their vigil, like all of Ted's endless Sunday tramping, scouring the hills, was in vain.

Queenie still lowed at dawn, demanding to be milked. The eagles still wheeled over the ridge. The tame grey lizard still came for crumbs in the morning. Jean ventured out from the house more than before; she learned from Ted how to rope and brand calves, and then to jerkily drive the cattle truck into town. Good as any man with stock, he told her boots. Nobody blamed her; nobody asked her to leave.

Perhaps, Jean reflected wryly, after three more summers had passed, perhaps May *was* a friend, after all.

*

It was two decades, and a new war in Korea come and gone, before the government letter arrived. *It has been determined by our engineering division.* Ted looked up from the Big Paddock at the hills to be sliced in half by the new highway. May began slamming doors. Soon bulldozers arrived, and men with dynamite. Ted scratched at his scalp. The jungled ridge belonged to the memory of Eric, not to the government. But then what if they turned something up. Hard to know what to think, really.

When the first young protesters came to the door, Ted walked away, but May dried her hands on a tea towel and listened. Don't bother the stock, she told them, and shut them bloody gates. A village of yurts and Kombis sprang up near the creek. Jean and Ted shook their heads. Girls in muslin dresses staggered up to the house, sunburnt, dehydrated, bitten by spiders. The trees are our brothers, Jean was informed by a boy who needed a lift to hospital the next day, concussed by a falling limb. A jolly fellow with an earring fell into the campfire and burned half his face off. At month's end, the remnant kernel of protesters tried, and failed, to scale the largest of the gum trees to stage a sit-in in its canopy.

It wasn't ultimately clear to the district who should bear the blame for the inferno. Most said the protesters, obviously, for lighting campfires in the first place, or May for allowing the city-bred fools on the property. Some blamed the cop who had deliberately kicked coals towards nylon tents, determined that the hippies be driven out. A few even blamed Ted for failing to maintain his rutted driveway better, so that the fire truck couldn't get to the paddock in time.

After the sirens had faded, and the night was at an end – the firefighters had picked up all their tools and taken them home, and the Kombis had all pulled away from the charred ground in disgrace – Ted, May and Jean slumped on the verandah, filthy and almost too tired for sleep. A profound silence fell upon the farm. No stock remained alive to bellow. The only sound was the faint shushing of a light breeze through the few pathetic trunks still standing in the blackened smear that was the Big Paddock. That, and a strange high tinkling from beyond the creek.

Bone-weary, Jean and May stared at each other. Then they ran, flinging great black clouds of ash in their wake. They forded the creek and ploughed their way through the fire-thinned scrub, until at last they stood below an enormous tallowwood, halfway up the mountain. It was a tree Ted knew; he had eaten a sandwich beneath it more than once on his Sunday treks. The fire had reached it, licked its trunk, caused it to shudder and tremble, but not to fall.

'There.'

Jean pointed up. Ted and May craned their necks, squinting in the first faint streak of dawn light. What tinkled above them was a narrow thread, dislodged from its resting place by the force of the fire, and spinning now in the breeze which blew across the empty paddock. The merest ghost of a belled ribbon, it had been wedged fast in the eagle's nest for thirty years.

Get me an axe, thought Jean.

Perry Feral

Allee Richards

This suburb has not that many trees. A few blocks away I can see
the orange neon sign – a petrol station. I pull the car over on the
side of a road. We sit in silence for almost a minute.

'So should I go then?' asks Corey.

'Whatever,' I say. I stare out the front windscreen and after a
while Corey leaves.

It's months since I last did this. I stopped doing this when I
started liking Claire and I started watching movies on Friday
nights with her and Corey instead of doing this. I only did this
once over that whole time, when Corey and Claire were in
Thailand.

Corey has never done this before. I used to go alone. Corey is
with me tonight because that's what brothers do in rom-coms
when one of them has a break-up – they go out together.

This is called petrol heading. I don't sniff petrol. This has
nothing to do with cars. This is finding a loner in a random suburb and pouring petrol on their head. Just the back, so it doesn't
go in their eyes or mouth, but it scares the shit out of them.
Really, it turns everyone into a pussy.

It's not the kind of thing Corey would usually do. When I first
told him about it he said no. He said I was fucked up. Said he
was going to tell Dad what I was doing. But I knew he wouldn't
actually tell Dad and Corey is always bored since Claire left so
here we are.

Waiting in the car for Corey to come back, I look up Claire on Facebook. Every time I do this I expect to see *Send Claire a friend request.* Meaning we're no longer friends. Meaning she deleted me. But this time, like every time, it says *Friends.* And there it is, her gummy smile.

The first time I ever saw Claire I walked in on them having sex. I wouldn't usually walk into Corey's room, that's not a thing we did, but I'd come home from the cannery and was going to ask Corey what he was making for dinner and I walked in on it, classic rom-com style. Corey's feet in odd socks at the bottom of the sheets and the back of Claire's torso and a bit of her crack above the sheets. Corey told me to get out and I remember standing in the doorway, not because I wanted to watch or because I even cared, but because I would stare at any stranger in the house whether they were making a cup of tea or cleaning the windows or fucking my brother. I don't remember if Dad was home.

Claire's blonde with one of those toothy smiles, like, you can see her gums, but she's hot. She always was out of Corey's league, but I think that was the point – she'd finished school and been to uni and was experimenting with dating a fuck-up.

Corey has lots of relationships, like a guy in a rom-com, he'll go to the shops and come home with a girlfriend. When Corey started working at the pub more girls started drinking there and they used to call him 'Ten'. He got fired, though, cos he was too dumb to polish glass.

I remember the first few nights Claire was at home watching TV with us – Dad, Corey and me. Claire asked questions during the ad breaks. She asked me about my last year at school and about work and about weekends. It was like she was interviewing me. Like we were the people on TV.

I don't remember her asking Dad any questions. He and Corey chewed chops silently in the background as the voices on the ads went '*down, down, down*'. I like ad breaks more than TV so at first found her annoying.

Corey's returned to the car holding only a packet of Twisties.

'I told you what to do,' I say.

'I forgot the jerry can,' he says, pulling the jerry can from under the passenger seat.

'Fuck it. I'll just go.' I take the can from him.

As soon as I walk in the fat cunt behind the counter says, 'Broken down?' He's looking at the jerry can.

'Yeah.'

'Where 'bouts?'

'Wilson Road.' Fat cunts always nod at 'Wilson Road', even if they don't know where it is, it sounds like a road everyone should know.

As I leave I take a newspaper without paying. That's against the rules. You should never give anybody in one of these towns a reason to remember you.

I put the jerry can full of petrol in the back seat and hand Corey the paper.

'What's the paper for?' he asks.

'The quiz.'

Corey opens the front page.

'The quiz is always at the back, moron,' I say.

'What three countries share a border with Thailand?' Corey reads.

'Laos,' I say.

'Cambodia, Burma, Malaysia.'

'It says three, dickhead.'

'I think it's four.'

'You think the quiz is wrong?'

'I don't know.'

'You went to Thailand with Claire.'

'I didn't go to the border.'

I use my phone to look up Thailand. This is how I used to do the quiz – never guessing, just finding the right answers straight up. Then Claire came along. There she was, standing in the kitchen on Saturday mornings looking between everyone – me, Corey and Dad – like we were spending time together. Like she thought we were a family on TV who spends time together in the kitchen. But really it was just that Dad was on the porch doing his copy of the quiz, and Corey was making breakfast in the kitchen, and I was on the computer looking up the answers for my own copy of the quiz, and all those things happened to be done near each other. Claire would drag me away from the computer. She said, 'It's no fun if you just look up the answers.' It was different for Claire; she had lots of good guesses to the questions.

'Fuck the quiz,' I say to Corey. 'Let's go.'

'But it's still really light,' he says.

'Let's just drive.'

I push too hard on the accelerator, the car lurches forward and the Twisties fall off Corey's lap, the yellow chips spill onto the floor.

'Pick that shit up!' I say.

'What the fuck is wrong with you?'

Corey doesn't get my joke. It was a reference to Dad. He mustn't remember. Or maybe he does, but he doesn't find it funny. Corey's weird like that.

This one time when I was, like, ten, I'd told Corey I could do it. He was jealous cos he was older than me and he couldn't do it. I went to my bed and wrapped myself in my doona. After I'd done it I found Corey in the lounge room sitting on the couch eating Twisties. I had my palm in a fist, like I was holding a bug in there. I opened my palm and showed him it. It looked like Clag and spit. Smelled milky, sweaty and dirty.

That's what it's always been like with Corey and me – even though I'm younger, I figured out how to jack it first. Corey didn't even tell me to fuck off, he just looked sad. Then Dad's shadow loomed over us like something off telly. Then Dad smacked my arm and the cum smeared on my cheek. Then Dad grabbed the bag of Twisties from Corey and threw those in the air. Dad had me by the shoulders, lifted off the floor, our noses were touching.

'Pick that shit up.' Dad kept his eyes right on me even though he was actually talking to Corey. Corey got on his hands and knees and collected the Twisties. Then Dad told us to both go outside. We sat on the porch and ate the dusty Twisties, which I remember made me really, really thirsty.

That night when Mum and Dad were screaming Dad said that if Corey and I were faggots he would kill her. That it was her fault if we were faggots.

I would've thought Corey would remember all that. I'd've thought he'd get my joke. Sometimes I wonder if Corey's some fucked-up retard.

*

I drive looking for a reserve or a patch of grass. I drive and it's like road, road, road. Streets with tens of concrete driveways like small roads leading to people's doors.

'Let's go somewhere else,' Corey says.

I turn the car around, making a big deal of the three-point turn, like a mum in a movie. I look for the biggest roads. The ones that look like they're leading to the biggest shops or the biggest parks.

'Seriously, nobody's around. Maybe people just don't go out here,' says Corey.

I yank at the steering wheel.

It's what all the rules are based on – somewhere, everywhere, anywhere there is always someone who works late so walks home late at night, or works in the day and walks their dog late at night, or exercises in the dark because they work in the day. And even without any of those people, everyone hates their kids anyway and wants to get away when it's dark. Somewhere, everywhere, anywhere, there is always someone walking alone.

These older guys from school had threatened to pour petrol on me once. They called themselves 'Petrol Heads', which is where I got the name. Looking back, I'm pretty sure they were just pussies.

I can see the supermarket's neon sign glowing above the houses. I drive towards the shining green light that's supposed to look like an apple. I'm coming for you, Big Apple.

'They're putting an ad online for entry levels next week,' Corey says. After a silence he adds, 'You said you wanted a job.'

'I said I wanted a trade.'

'Work is work.'

'Dad said he'd ask Bill to give me a trade.'

'Yep.' Corey sounds sad, which is probably because he can't get a trade cos he's not tough; he's more pussy than blokey.

Dad says that in the meantime, until Bill can give me work, it's good to work at the cannery. He says I should learn how to work before I get a proper job.

I wonder if Dad asked Bill ages ago and Bill said no and Dad's not telling me.

I wonder if Dad never asked Bill.

It was Claire who first suggested I get a job with Corey.

I remember because she called his work 'the call centre' and I'd never heard it called that before; Corey always called it 'the office'.

'There's a pub, let's go there,' says Corey. I'm not sure if he means instead of petrol heading or if he means to pass the time until it's dark enough to petrol head. We can't go to the pub because we can't give anyone a reason to remember us, so I park the car near a pier and we get high – joints, not the petrol. After only two or three drags I start laughing at things that aren't here. I think about Perry Feral. Huh, huh.

*

The first time I liked Claire was the first time I found her funny. We were watching TV and it was an ad break and the news came on and the newsreader was a small chick with a big bun on her head, the kind of bun you only see on TV and mostly on newsreaders. She was reading the news and then she said 'peripheral' except she said it like two words like 'perry' then 'feral'. She quickly apologised, still in the newsreader voice, and said it properly, 'peripheral'.

Claire pretended to be the newsreader. She put on an American accent even though the newsreader wasn't American and said, 'This is Perry Feral reporting live!'

I cracked up. Dad said 'huh', just once. Corey tried to say 'perry' then 'feral' with an American accent, but he sounded dumb. Claire and I laughed. I'd never met a girl who was funny before Claire.

Claire was good at American accents. One time we were having dinner, Corey put a plate of barbecued meat on the coffee table and I lifted a steak with my fork. I was holding this huge bit of meat on the end of my fork and I said, 'This is one huuuu-uge bit of meat.'

I remember Claire leaning all her weight on one leg, pushing her hips to the side; she held each of her arms out and in an American accent she said, 'Huge.' It was a reference to Julia Roberts in *Pretty Woman*.

Corey and I cracked up. Dad turned the sound up on the TV. That's what I used to do on Friday nights when I found Claire

funny, I stopped petrol heading and we watched rom-coms –
Corey, Claire and I. Dad was at the pub.

Claire had learned how to watch telly by then. She'd understood that you only talk to make fun of someone on the TV. And
that's how I realised how funny rom-coms can be.

Claire hated Katherine Heigl the most, so we watched a lot of
her movies. We laughed a lot. It was a real barrel of laughs. Even
Corey got the jokes, not like now. Corey sort of got things more
when Claire was around. I used to hate watching rom-com movies, because my ex-girlfriend didn't realise they're supposed to
be funny.

I wonder if Mum ever made Dad watch rom-coms.

I wonder if Mum knew they were funny, or if she watched
them seriously like other girls.

*

Corey and I are still in the car, getting high, watching waves still
lapping on the pier.

'Shit,' says Corey. He's staring at a cop who's staring at us.

'Pussy.' I run my lighter up and down my joint even though it's
lit. The pig walks to the car with heaps of pretend swagger. He
reaches the driver-side window and stands, looking at us in the
car. I take a drag of the joint. He knocks a knuckle on my window. I wind it down, but don't turn to face him. I exhale the
smoke fast and hard, the way we used to spit water when we were
kids. It hits the windscreen then floats out the open window. The
pig just stands there watching.

'Stare bear,' I say.

Corey cracks up, but then he tries to keep his mouth closed,
which sort of makes him sound like an actual pig.

'Time to move on, mate,' says the pig.

'There's two of us,' I say. 'Mate-sssssssss.'

'Time to move on.'

'It's illegal to drive stoned.'

'Yeah,' says Corey.

'Just leave and don't cause any trouble.'

'Nah,' I say.

'Are you going to cause trouble?' the pig asks.

'Nah,' I say.

'So just leave.'

'I can't be fucked.' I finally look the pig in the eye.

The first time I saw a pig was not that long after Mum had left. A small bit of time when Dad was around a lot. I was lying on the floor beneath my bedroom window. The pig's voice travelled in from the front doorstep.

'Why is that, Mr Ashton?' he said.

I walked from my bedroom to our entranceway. The cop and a lady standing at the door both looked at me, which made Dad turn around. He scooped his arm, like he was calling me nearer. I walked until I was as close as two steps behind Dad. He put his hand on my shoulder and pulled me into his leg, the only time I can remember that happening.

'I just can't be fucked.' Dad was staring at the cop and the lady. The cop and the lady were staring at me.

The pig watches us as we drive away from the pier. Never do anything to make anybody remember you. We blew it.

'At least he didn't arrest us,' says Corey.

'He couldn't arrest us. It's not illegal to sit in a car. He just wishes he lived in America and we were black,' I say.

'That lady at school said I should be a cop,' says Corey.

'Don't.'

'Why?'

'Bros don't let bros become cops,' I say. I accidentally stall the car, then I stall it again on purpose.

'Do you reckon if you met Claire and she wasn't my girlfriend that you'd fuck her?' asks Corey. It's random cos it's the first time he's talked about Claire since they broke up.

'Yeah,' I say.

'Did you fuck her?' he asks.

'She was your girlfriend.'

*

I remember Claire asking me if I wanted a girlfriend. She told me about girls at the call centre and dating apps that were 'cool now'.

'I don't want a girlfriend,' I said, which was true. All my girl-friends at school either had fucked-up lives or if they didn't they would tell me how fucked up my life was.

'You're not even thinking about it. Just imagine it for a second,' said Claire.

Corey was cooking pancakes in the kitchen behind us. It was late at night. I think this must have been after we watched *The Notebook* because they cook pancakes late at night in *The Notebook* and we were probably having such a shit conversation cos the movie was so not funny.

Claire went on, 'You could have one arm around her and you'd be cruising 'round.' Claire held an arm to the side pretending she had a chick there. She held her other arm in front of her, hand in a fist, pretending she was driving.

'I don't have a car,' I said.

'You're not even pretending! Pretend at least, Easy!' Claire used to call me Easy.

Corey's pan hissed and he waved his spatula in front of his face.

'If I had a girlfriend I'd fucking crash the car,' I said.

'Ian.' Claire stared at me like chick teachers at school used to stare at me. 'Ian, that's not funny.'

'Has Corey ever hit you?' I asked.

'What?' Immediately she wasn't pissed at me anymore.

'Has he ever hit you?'

'Why would you ask me that?'

I stared at her and we were quiet for a bit.

'Has Corey hit someone before?' asked Claire.

I left a pause before I said anything. 'Nah.'

'Then why are you asking?'

'One in every fifty men hit their partners.'

'Ian.'

'It was in the quiz last week.'

*

It's dark now. We've found the main street. The main street, the main event. Huh, huh.

'Should we go to a strip club?' asks Corey.

'Together?'

'Yeah.'

'Faggot.'

'There's chicks there.'

I park the car and grab my backpack from behind the seat.

'Dude, we can't do this anymore,' says Corey.

'We talked about this yesterday,' I say.

'Nah, that cop copied down the numberplate.'

'He didn't copy down shit.'

'Are you sure?'

'Yeah, I saw him.'

Corey grabs his backpack and follows me out of the car. We walk past a shop that sells pizza and souvlakis. Inside young people are wiping down tables and mopping the floor.

'I've never seen a stripper,' says Corey.

'What are you obsessed with them for?' I ask.

'I'm single now.'

He has a point. Some guys in rom-coms do go to strip clubs, broken-hearted guys and arseholes.

'You don't even care that you guys broke up.'

'Yeah.'

Behind the takeaway shop and the Big Apple, there's a roundabout. It's a more exposed spot than is ideal, but it is grassy. We sit facing the back door of the pizza and souva shop. The dumpster next to the door is graffitied, *Stay high forever.*

'Fuck yeah. Motherfucker.' Corey nods to the dumpster as he lights another joint.

*

They broke up because that's what couples do when they're not in movies. I watched them talking in the backyard from the porch. They spoke quietly, like two people speaking in a waiting room. Even the clothesline that was being pushed by the breeze was louder. *Squeak*, as it went in a circle.

Nobody yelled. Nobody said they didn't understand. Nobody said someone did something that somebody hadn't done. Nobody said much but a few quiet words as Dad's paint-stained overalls rotated on the line behind them.

When Mum and Dad broke up there was screaming. I remember I crawled out of bed to the hallway that was full of the sound.

I remember taking slow steps, one at a time, like that dopey walk people do down the aisle at weddings. I remember I opened their door and I remember Mum on the bedroom floor, knees and thighs together, feet angled outward behind her. Hunched shoulders, her hair over her face, like a broken mermaid. I remember Dad staring at me standing in the doorway of his room.

Maybe that wasn't exactly the time Mum and Dad broke up, but just another one of their arguments. Sometimes I'd hear the screams travelling down the hall, like a protest coming at me. I remember Mum walking into my room and Dad standing in my doorway, pleading with her to go back to their room. He used her name – Louise. That happened a few times and then one time Dad stood there in my bedroom door and served her one in front of me and after that Mum never walked into my room again.

She left not long after. Forever, that is. It's a better way to go, I think. Wait till things are so fucked up that when you do breakup everyone is like, fuck yes!

Corey and Claire were together and then they weren't. It just ended. Claire was around and then she wasn't anymore. No fuss. Like someone deciding they would die and just walking out to the backyard and gradually disappearing. No funeral.

I left the porch and I sat in the lounge room. I didn't turn on the TV, but sat alone on the couch staring at the blank screen. I thought about crying. I thought, fuck that. Before Claire left the house for the last time she said, 'It's okay. I'll still see you.'

That was months ago. Fucking bitch.

'Dude, I told you, nobody comes out here,' says Corey.

There is no one out, which means that if someone comes out now they'll be perfect. Only petrol head when nobody else can see you.

'There was a guy before,' I say.

'That was ages ago and nobody has come out since then, he must be the only one that works there,' says Corey. 'Let's just get high.'

'We are high.'

'But let's do it somewhere else.'

'Let's wait for the cop to come by.'

Eventually three guys walk out of the shop's back door. Corey shuffles onto his stomach like he's trying to hide in the grass even though it's freshly mown. The guys talk and light cigarettes next to the dumpster and then they split. Two walk one way and one goes in another direction. I go for the pair.

'Dude, what are you doing?' Corey asks.

I'd told him we should only ever go for a loner. Corey is following me anyway.

I reach the two dudes and they turn and look at me and I look at them. I shake the jerry can, thrusting it forward in the air. They start running and I try to run after them, but it's too hard when both hands are holding something above your head. I throw the can at one of their retreating backs and I yell to them, 'I have a match. I have a lighter. I'm gunna fucking light you on fire!' I've never said that to anybody. It was never in the script before.

The guys just run. And Corey is running far the other way. The sounds of the guys' steps and of Corey's are retreating, becoming fainter in different directions. And then I run.

I think – I'm going to run as long as I can feel the cold bitumen smacking my feet. Forever I'm gunna hear it thud, thud, thud, thud.

One of the guys looks back and sees me following and he shits himself a bit and then the other guy shits himself a bit too, as in they're both running faster. So I run faster because they're running faster and because I bet they've fucked off on someone before in their lives and it's like what goes around comes around or some bullshit and I'm coming for you pussies.

Corey pulls up in the car beside me.

'Easy,' Corey says. 'Easy, mate.'

Thud, thud, thud, becomes *scuff, scuff, scuff.*

The Wall

Julie Koh

On morning TV, a politician is promising to build a wall. The wall will divide Australia across the middle.

'It's a wall to keep the Chinese out,' the politician explains. 'Every night the tiny Chinese people come in and stroke my hair as I sleep. It's illegal. They expect to get paid well for all the stroking – discount prices, they say. I tell them this isn't a free country. We don't just hand out jobs. If you disagree, you're on the wrong side of the wall.'

As the politician takes more questions, a wrecking ball swings through our bedroom. It takes out the TV with a crash.

The dust settles. I peer out from the wreckage into the front yard. Men in short shorts and boots are already dismantling the letterbox and driving stakes into the ground. From the way the stakes are arranged, I can see that the wall is going to be built right down the middle of our marital bed.

'Excuse me,' I say. 'You can't build that wall through my *house*.'

'You should have told the inquiry that,' says one of the men. 'You should have put in a submission.'

'My husband will have something to say about this,' I tell them, but he is nowhere to be found.

It is afternoon before I hear from him.

'Darling, can you hear me?' he shouts from the other side of the wall.

'Thank God you're okay!' I shout back.

'Which button do I press to start the washing machine?'

I look around me. I realise that in the division, I didn't get the laundry or the bathroom or the kitchen, or even the garden taps.

By sunset, I can't hold my pee in any longer. I squat in the backyard under the lemon tree, contemplating the wall.

It has left my side in total shade.

In time, my clothes start to stink. I don't have money for the laundromat. I toss clothes over the wall to my husband. I can hear them land, but they never come back.

I shout to ask him if he's washed them.

'What clothes?' he yells.

'The pink coat with the white birds? The blue skirt with the yellow tulips?'

The guard on our section of the wall looks over at my husband's side.

'I don't see any laundry,' he says, adjusting the sling on his rifle. 'We don't see any laundry.'

I try to write a complaint to the government. I sit down with a pen and paper but can't get the words right. There is too much noise on the other side of the wall. Construction work during the day, but other noises too.

Thump, thump, thump.

My husband must have bought a treadmill. I call out to him but he doesn't answer.

I wonder where he is running.

The next day, as I prune the wilting bushes in the front yard, the local newspaper lands in a roll at my feet.

The front page says: 'All in Thrall of Great Wall'. Men in hard hats and ties grin out at me.

As the days progress, wall-related articles retreat further back into the paper.

One morning, buried on page thirty-seven, I read the headline 'Local Couple Having a Wall of a Time'. The article features a photo of my husband with his arm around a woman who has the skin of a baby.

She is wearing a pink coat with white birds, and a blue skirt with yellow tulips.

Behind them is their half of the house, newly renovated. The grass in the photo is green and lush, and has grown into a vast front meadow filled with blue flowers.

The wall is covered in a thick layer of cork. I decide that it will work well as a vision board.

I cut out the picture from the newspaper and pin it to my board: an achievement unachieved.

I think about the wall every waking hour.

I hover near it, watching it.

I fall asleep next to it with my right hand splayed against its surface.

My husband on the other side doesn't do the same back. He pounds eternally against a body that isn't mine, in the midst of a glorious meadow.

Slut Trouble

Beejay Silcox

The first girl is taken on the second weekend of the school holidays. Her name is Julie-Anne Marks; she is nineteen, she is beautiful, and she is gone. Everywhere we look Julie-Anne Marks is looking back at us. Just the one photo at first – the one her parents gave the police the night she didn't come home. Julie-Anne Marks is stuffed into our letterboxes, pinned to every bulletin board, taped to every telephone pole. She takes up the whole front page of *The Messenger* – a full page in colour, block-capital headline. WHERE IS OUR JULIE-ANNE?

'Don't you just love her hair?' Megan asks me. And I do, I do. People are always mistaking Megan and me for sisters because of our hair. We wear it the same way now, and from the back you can't tell us apart. Every morning before school I call Megan on the kitchen phone and she tells me what I need to do to match her – French braid, fishtail, high pony. If I listen closely, I can hear the phone ringing in her house next door, the drum-roll clatter of her running down the stairs to answer.

We are cursed with boring hair, straight and house-mouse brown. It won't hold a curl or a crimp for longer than an hour, and neither of us has been allowed to dye it: my mum says I'm too young; Megan's dad – Mr Henderson – says it looks cheap and nasty. The only thing it does is grow, so Megan and I are having a competition to see whose will be the longest by the end of the year. Six months ago we had it cut the same length. Megan made the hairdresser measure it exactly, and neither of us has touched it since. Megan is winning, which is how she likes it.

Julie-Anne's hair is wild and thick, near-black with a wink of red where the sun hits it. It's the colour of blackberry jam or red wine. Mr Henderson lets each of us have a half tumbler of red wine when I sleep over, so long as we promise not to tell anyone. He joined a wine club last year after Mrs Henderson left and has been trying to teach us how to taste all of the different flavours – wet leather, smoke, dried leaves. We never can, but we don't want to hurt his feelings, so we just sip and nod, until he gives up and waves us away. Later, after he falls asleep on the couch, we slink out of Megan's bedroom and finish whatever we can find that's left open – he can never keep track. We pour it into the good glasses her Mum forgot to take, and make up our own language for the bitterness.

'Can you taste the … halitosis in this, Laura?'

'I can, Megan, I can. And is that an undertone of armpit?'

'I don't know if it's armpit, but close, perhaps a touch of gangrene?'

'Of course, it's gangrene! Silly me. And with an aftershock of fingernail clippings.'

'You are so right, Laura – that's the flavour that catches in the back of your throat.'

Julie-Anne's parents and not-a-suspect boyfriend hold a press conference where they cling to each other and weep and beg for her safe return. The people they interview on the news – her university lecturers, the boss of the café where she works – say the most wonderful things about her: so kind, so caring, so gentle. Such a good girl, an honest-to-god angel. We have no trouble believing them. Just look at that wide-open face. Beautiful. There's no better word for it. Julie-Anne Marks is beautiful, and everyone is looking for her.

Megan unpins a poster from the jacaranda that stands watch between her house and mine. *Do you know something?* Another appears. The flier is printed on expensive paper with a colour photo of Julie-Anne sitting cross-legged on a picnic blanket. She's wearing cut-off denim shorts and an oversized flannel shirt with the sleeves rolled up. *Did you see something?* The blanket is mustard yellow with a print of blue flowers. Her shirt is checked grey and black, with a wide rust-orange diagonal stripe. You can tell it's a man's shirt, because the buttons are on the wrong side. *Can you help?* Her feet are bare, toenails unpainted. She's pointing at something off to the right, but you can't see what it is. What you can see is that Julie-Anne wasn't expecting the camera: her eyes are too wide, her mouth too open. You can't fake that look, no matter how hard you try.

We iron the poster flat and slip Julie-Anne Marks inside the stiff cover of Megan's old copy of *Possum Magic*. We get into trouble for hacking the legs from last winter's jeans to make shorts. We wear them every day.

The Mackenzies across the road are the only family on our block who get the thick city paper delivered every morning, but they don't pick it up until they get home from work. Megan dares me to steal it.

'Can't we just ask if we can have it after they're finished?'

'When did you get so fucking boring?' Megan drags the F word out. She's only just started to say it, and is still enjoying the new taste of it. I can't bring myself to say it out loud, but at night I mouth it in the dark before I go to sleep. Fuck. Fucking. Fuck you. Fuck off.

Megan keeps watch while I run across the road and onto the Mackenzies' lawn. I can feel her watching me.

'You run like a spaz,' she says as I hand her the paper.

I hold it still while Megan slides the Julie-Anne pages out slowly so they don't rip. We stuff the rest of the paper in Dr Barker's bin next door while Titus the terrible terrier scolds us through the fence. There's a whole section devoted to Julie-Anne, even a page of photos set out like a yearbook spread. Here is Julie-Anne holding her sister's baby; at the beach in her surf lifesaving uniform; high-school graduation with her cap and gown. Here is Julie-Anne kissing the cheek of her adorable boyfriend, and don't they look so happy?

'I would absolutely fuck him,' Megan says, though neither of us has had a boyfriend yet, or any idea what it would be like to have one. Mum hasn't had one since Dad died, so I couldn't ask her, even if I wanted to. Mrs Henderson does have one, but Megan's never met him – though she did see him once, a year ago, lifting her mum's cheetah-print suitcase into the back of his car. Mrs

Henderson has only visited twice since, and always on her own. Last time she told me to call her Lisa, but I couldn't. Megan does.

Megan is bored. Her room is boring. Her house is boring. TV is boring. I am boring. We build a tent in the far corner of my yard out of an old wool blanket and an ocky strap strung between the lemon tree and the back fence. We drag the guest bedroom mattress out across the grass and fill the tent with Megan's mum's fancy throw pillows – all velvet and tassel. Mr Henderson says he's glad to see them gone, that they made him feel like he was living in a house of ill repute.

We spend the day out in the tent sucking on ice cubes of frozen cordial, reading about Julie-Anne and listening to the *Grease* soundtrack on my Walkman. When school starts up next year, they'll be casting for the musical. Megan is going to try out for Sandra Dee, or maybe Rizzo. She can't decide. We have to be careful to keep the cassette out of the sun; if it gets too hot, the tape inside will warp and snap. In the afternoon heat we slip into a thick syrupy sleep. Filtered through our blanket roof, the sun fills the tent with an underwater blue. I wake before Megan and watch her in the glow, her hair mermaid-loose across the pillows, lips green from the Cottee's. She looks so cold.

Megan dreams of Julie-Anne Marks. In these dreams Julie-Anne is sitting on the picnic blanket, and Megan is taking her picture. Julie-Anne points off to the right, but when Megan tries to look, she wakes up.

'She's trying to tell me something, Laura.'

'Do you think she's pointing at him?'

'I don't know, but she's definitely still alive, I can feel it. He's keeping her prisoner somewhere because he's fallen in love with her.'

'Like in *Beauty and the Beast*?'

'Exactly!'

I know she's lying, and she knows I know. When Megan is lying she straightens her back and tilts her chin up like she's the queen. She dictates these dreams to me, and it is my job to write them down in case she is secretly psychic and some tiny detail is a clue that will lead the police to Julie-Anne. We take turns practising what we would say to the TV people if we found her.

'I'm so glad she's alive,' I say.

'Is that the best you can do? Glad? That's a nothing word. You wouldn't be glad.'

'Happy?'

'Honestly, Laura, try harder.' Megan puts her hand over her heart like she's about to sing 'Advance Australia Fair'. 'Me? A hero? You're so kind to say, but I'm just so grateful that I was able to play even a small part in bringing Julie-Anne home safe.'

Megan and I go shopping. I have birthday money from Grandma Bailey and Megan has 'Lisa's Lousy Guilt Cash'. Her mum has sent her a card with five dollars in it every month since she left. We buy flannel shirts from Men's World – not the same as Julie-Anne's, but as close as we can find. We change into them in the shopping centre bathroom and stare into the mirror too long, hoping to catch just the smallest hint of Julie-Anne in our own faces. We compare the length of our hair.

'I've caught up!' I say, and it is true, mine is longest. I realise too late how stupid I have been to say it.

'Who cares?'

'There's still time left, you could still ...'

'I don't give a shit, Laura.'

'It was your idea.'

'Did you really think I was serious? Are you really that fucking dumb?'

'I guess not.'

'That shirt doesn't even suit you.'

'But what about you?' I ask. 'We look the same. We look like sisters.'

'But we're not.' Megan yells over her shoulder as she walks out.

Megan doesn't speak to me again until lunch. We are sitting at a table in the food court, silently eating our chips, when I see a woman who looks like a Julie-Anne impersonator. She isn't quite as beautiful, but she has the same red darkness in her hair, the same generous smile. I point her out and Megan and I are friends again.

'I bet this is how he found her,' she turns to me and whispers, 'I bet he just saw her one day and couldn't help but follow her. I bet it was love at first sight.'

We follow her. We follow her from the bathroom to Books-Books-Books where she wanders through the aisles, running her fingertips across the spines like they're harp strings. We peek at her from behind open magazines like we are movie spies. We follow her into the fancy perfume section of the chemist, where all the jewelled bottles have one-word names: Escape, Seduction, Heat, Romance, Obsessed. We follow her into Woolies and watch as she chooses fancy cheeses and a bag of red apples, glossy as lipstick. We follow her out and down into the underground car park until we have her alone. Our sneakers squeak; our stifled laughter spills. She never notices us.

'See how easy it would be?' Megan asks, as we watch her drive away.

The second girl is taken on the day that would have been my parents' seventeenth wedding anniversary. Her name is Kimberly Watson. Mum is driving us back from the video store when the news comes on the radio. We learn that Kimberly Watson was twenty-two – an aspiring actress who was last seen outside a bar called Club Exotique, hopping into a taxi.

'Bloody stupid girl,' Mum says. She changes the station as we wait at the lights.

Now it is Kimberly Watson's face all over the telly. Her first photo is a close-up in black and white. She's staring into the camera with a smile that's pulled tight as a mousetrap; eyelids dark and smudged like she is sliding out of focus.

'I don't like that photo,' I say. 'She's trying too hard.'

'It's not a photo, it's a headshot, dumb arse,' Megan says. She knows about these kinds of things.

Mr Henderson says that only sluts get into the kind of trouble Kimberly Watson has clearly gotten herself into.

'What kind of trouble is that?' I ask him.

'Slut trouble, Laura, slut trouble.'

I ask my mum about slut trouble, and she suggests that movie nights should be at our place from now on.

After Kimberly Watson, the summer becomes claustrophobic. Megan and I aren't allowed to go anywhere on our own, not even down to the park, or the deli at the corner – definitely not to the beach. Mr Henderson spends a whole weekend building a gate into the fence between our houses so that we don't have to walk out onto the street to see each other. Megan and I beg our parents to be allowed to sleep in the tent at night. It's sticky and hot under our blanket's blue roof, but late in the evening the smothering air starts to stir as the sea breeze comes in, and the tent sucks the air in and out like it is breathing. We sleep deeply and wake with the sun, our hair snarled with bottlebrush spikes and the thin sharp leaves from the peppermint tree.

Kimberly Watson's family doesn't cry. Her father clenches his jaw so tight you can almost hear his teeth squeak. Her mother stares off to the side of the room, but her eyes don't catch on anything. She reminds me of one of those fish you can buy propped up on the slush behind the meat counter. Kimberly's twin brother reads a statement. You can see the echo of Kimberly in his face, but in him it's more handsome.

'I'd fuck him,' I say, but Megan pretends not to notice.

'She deserves whatever she gets,' Megan says.

I'm not sure exactly how the game starts, but Megan is in charge. We play it in the tent, at night once my mum turns the house lights off. Megan is Julie-Anne and I am him. To get into character, Megan coils her limp rope of hair under a black wig from an old witch costume and wears her flannel shirt. I wear a brown suit jacket that smells of Mr Henderson – wet leather, dried leaves, smoke.

We stand together in the tent and I say: 'You are the most beautiful creature I have ever seen, Julie-Anne Marks. I love you, and I must have you,' and press a chloroformed handkerchief to her mouth (it's a tea towel sprayed with some of my mum's drugstore perfume). Megan swoons to the mattress.

The rules are simple: he can do whatever he likes to her. If she moves, she loses. If Megan laughs or squirms or opens her eyes, the game is over and we start again, but this time she is him and I am Kimberly Watson. I am not allowed to be Julie-Anne. There is no point in arguing.

When I am Kimberly, I wear one of the dresses that Megan's mum left behind – an itchy black thing with massive shoulder pads and two rows of gold buttons down the front the size of honky nuts. When I am Kimberly all he says is: 'Slut.' I do not swoon. I am pushed.

At first it is easy to win. We tickle, stick tongues in ears and fingers up noses, whisper the grossest words we know (booger, fanny, sperm, tampon, fallopian) and that's all it takes before we are both lost – curled up together on the mattress, our laughter loud and loose. Titus complains from behind the fence. Our stomachs ache from holding the laughter in. But on the third night the words aren't funny anymore. We are no longer ticklish.

I am him, and Megan can't, won't be stirred. She is lying on her back with her arms up above her head. In the moon-dark the wig looks like her real hair. Her head is tilted back, her eyes are closed and in that moment, I can see her – I can see Julie-Anne. Perfect, beautiful Julie-Anne in Megan's mean little face. I hate her. I fucking hate her. I stand over her and stomp one foot down onto her belly fast and hard. Catch the sharp, lurking edge of her hip against the heel of my foot. She makes a strange, animal noise and curls onto her side away from me.

'I beat you,' I say, 'you lose.' She refuses to speak, but stands, pulls off the wig and shakes out her hair. I unbutton the jacket. It is my turn.

I am ready for her to hurt me.

'Slut.'

She pushes me to the mattress and sits on my stomach. She moves heavily – drives the air out of me. The dress buttons press against my ribs. I feel her weight shift and she slaps me hard. I keep my eyes closed. Say nothing. I can feel her body tightening and I know she is going to slap me again. It hurts less the second time.

She slides herself down so she is pinning my knees and leans over me. Her hair falls across my eyelids. I can almost taste her strawberry shampoo. I can feel her undoing the giant buttons of Lisa's dress and opening it up, and then the smaller buttons of my nightie, too. The tent fills with the new sour-milk smell of my sweat. There is only dark against my skin – the dark and her heavy eyes. It's not cold, but my skin bucks and prickles as she runs her fingertips in slow loops down over my face and throat and nipples and ribs, and then up again and deep into my hair. Again, again, but this time she drags her bitten nails down my belly and hooks her fingers into the waistband of my knickers. I wait. She snaps the elastic. Once. Twice.

'You reek,' she spits at me, as she pushes herself up and leaves the tent.

I know this is a test. And so I wait. I hear the gate in the fence thump open, and the back door of the Henderson house. I wait.

There is ocean in the air now – the night is chilling and I'm pressing myself tight into the mattress to hold the shiver. I am waiting. I listen to the cicadas and the crickets, the garden's insect heartbeat. Everything seems louder, the smell of the chloroformed rag, the sheep-stink of the wool, the crushed leaves of the peppermint tree. I am waiting for him. And I know now with a cold and magnificent certainty that even after this game is over a part of me will always be waiting.

Help Me Harden My Heart

Dominic Amerena

I'm scrubbing the word SCUM off the front door of our house. I wipe so hard that my wrists start to ache, but the red letters remain bold and bright, their edges dripping as if they're bleeding.

The whipbirds are going mad in the fig tree by the fence, the way they always do before a storm. I turn and look at the dark clouds collecting over the buildings in the CBD. We live on the court up the top of Mount Coot-tha. Our view stretches all the way down through Toowong to the big bend in the Brisbane River, dishwater grey in the gathering gloom.

Inside people are moving around, slamming cupboard doors. I can hear their muffled voices in the living room. I lean my forehead against the door, against the red, dripping letters. The fumes from the turps are making me light-headed. I stay very still and I breathe deeply, again and again, trying to stop myself remembering.

Last night I was standing by our bedroom window, watching the Christmas lights on our neighbour's roof. I heard Karl sit up in bed and start to sob. Eventually he swung his legs over the side of the bed and tried to stand, but he'd forgotten about his broken foot and crumpled facedown on the carpet. He lay still. I thought he'd passed out, but when I crouched down beside him and ran my fingers through his hair I could hear him making this wet, barely there sound, a kind of whimpering, as though his lungs were full of water.

Once I'd gotten him back in bed I tried to feed him the sleeping pills Dr Joyce had prescribed, but he kept coughing them back up. Eventually I crushed the tablets into a longneck and fed it to him in sips between his sobs, the same way I used to feed Seth his formula when he was a toddler.

I'd finally got Karl down when I heard a car pull up out the front of the house. The sound of doors slamming and an engine ticking over. I heard the creak of our front gate and their boots on the path. Their voices were thick with drink as they walked along the verandah. I listened to a can rattling and the paint being sprayed across the door.

I was going to make a dash for the phone in the hallway to call the police, but I just stood there frozen, waiting for them to come through the front door and do whatever they'd come here to do. Looking back on it, I was almost thankful for the fear, I was thankful to not be thinking about him for a few moments. They finished spraying and I heard the sound of their piss hissing on the welcome mat, their voices fading into the night.

*

I must have got turps in my eyes, because they're burning. I blink furiously and dab at them with the sleeve of my shirt, fumble the front door open and rush down the hall, making sure not to look into the living room. I make it to the bathroom, turn the sink's taps on full. It's only when the water hits my face that I realise I'm just crying again.

The mirror's still flecked with toothpaste. Seth would always make a terrible mess when he cleaned his teeth. He brushed with incredible force, flicking toothpaste all over the sink and the mirror, the bathroom tiles. He brushed like he was trying to hurt himself, like he was trying to destroy something. The mess he made used to drive me mad, but since he left I haven't been able to bring myself to clean it.

'Mrs Kenny.' It's one of the agent's voices, coming from the doorway. I try to block him out, to concentrate on my reflection in the mirror. I notice the search warrant balled in the front pocket of my shirt.

'Mrs Kenny?' He says my name like it hurts. 'We need you.'

I follow him down the hallway towards the living room. His suit's too hot for the weather and continents of sweat are spreading out from his armpits, from the small of his back.

My son's teeth are spread out across our coffee table. The agent with the front rower's neck is sitting on our couch taking photos with one of those big crime scene cameras that you see on the telly. Even though some of them have been sitting there for a decade or so, the teeth are still white, like life hasn't got to them yet.

'We're taking these,' he says, counting them into an evidence bag. 'They will be used as evidence —'

'Can I keep one?' I say, in a strange, tiny voice.

'Once the body has been identified the teeth will be returned to you.'

'One. I only want one. Please let me keep one.'

I'm still saying please, as they usher me over to the couch, shove a glass of water into my hand. They confer in low voices by the living room door, and then one of them approaches me with the evidence bag, holds it open before me like a lucky dip.

'Just one.' He gives me a tight-lipped, toothless smile. His partner rams his phone to his ear, walks out the front door.

I put my hand in the bag, run my fingers through his teeth, those brittle little memories. The tooth I choose is an incisor, fine and long, with a pointed tip. I slip it into my bra.

The agent is looking at me like I've gone mad as he takes the evidence bag off me. I follow him to the front door. He tells me to expect a call as soon as the remains have been analysed. He tells me that I should know by tonight. Through our bedroom door Karl's snoring is like water going down a drain. As the agent talks I nod, all the while looking at the words JIHAD SCUM scrawled across our front door.

*

I'm lying on my side on the living room rug, switching telly stations whenever a news bulletin comes on. Time has operated strangely since Seth left. Sometimes it feels like every second's being seared into me. Other times whole days will pass without me even noticing. I'll be sitting at the kitchen table and the light will change outside and I'll realise that I've been there for hours.

The phone rings. I urge myself to pick up, to get it over with, but it clicks over to the answering machine, and there's Audrey's voice saying that she's at the supermarket on her way home from work and asking what groceries I need.

The old recording was Seth saying: 'We might be in, we might be out, but leave a message and you'll find out!' We recorded it when he was just starting Year Nine. Karl was still working in the mines outside Mount Isa, and Seth and I were alone in the house. I wrote the message out for him and begged him to read it into the machine. I suppose I wanted us to sound like a happy family. He read it in his soft, stumbling voice, often pausing between the words. It sounded like he was apologising for something he'd done wrong.

Karl and I erased the message after they started playing it on the news, trying to match it to the hooded figure's voice on the videos. By that stage Seth had been gone for a week and we already knew he wasn't coming home.

The press had got hold of the blog he put online after he made it to Syria. They were already coming up with nicknames for him: The Tropical Terrorist. Sicko Seth. The police had taken Seth's computer, but we managed to get the blog up on the iPad. We read it sitting on the side of the bed, our backs to the window, trying to ignore the journalists milling about in the front yard.

It was full of isms. Terrorism and patriotism and atheism and capitalism. It was full of threats against the kids and teachers at his school. But there were Seth's spelling errors too, his childlike turns of phrase. He called those hooded men in the desert his best mates, he called them cool and awesome. He said they were the only ones who 'know what I'm about'.

Last year Seth would sit with us while we were watching the news. When a report came on showing those men firing guns into the air, he'd say things like, 'One man's terrorist is another man's freedom fighter' or 'The government is trying to pull the wool over our eyes'. He'd say the words tentatively, like he was feeling how they sounded coming out of his mouth. He'd look at me while he spoke, to see if I was reacting. We thought it was just stuff he'd picked up in Media Studies. We were just glad he was showing an interest. We suggested journalism courses for him to study at uni, once he'd finished school.

When I saw the videos on the news, I knew it was him of course. I recognised his voice immediately: the stuttered starts of his sentences, the way he softened his r's into w's. Rhotacism, the speech pathologist called it. Rhotacism, expressive language disorder, anhedonic tendencies. Since Seth was born, Karl and I have become fluent in the language of dysfunction, all those long, cold words trying to classify his sadness.

He was a quiet child, turned in on himself. He went around with a permanently pained expression, as if he was missing a layer of skin. We sent him to counsellors for a while, but none of them seemed to make him any better.

Once Karl got laid off from his job in the mines, we couldn't afford the therapy. 'He's just a late bloomer,' Karl said. 'This is probably the best thing for him. He'll be fine.'

The storm's mucking with the signal of the TV now, and the screen's showing a scrambled image from a vacuum cleaner ad with the slogan, 'For When Life Sucks'. Seth used to help me get the TV working. He was always good with electronics, things with screens and buttons, things he didn't have to talk to. Sometimes I'd put all the cables in the wrong sockets at the back of the set-top box, just so I had an excuse to speak with him.

I go into the bedroom to check on Karl. He's on his back, staring up at the ceiling with the half-drunk longneck beside the bed. He looks ridiculous with his whippet chest, the big, clunky moon boot. Karl's always been a runner, but after Seth left, that's all he did. He'd run down from Chapel Hill across the river and all the way out to Oxley. He'd run through the night, out to Brisbane's city limits and back, until he got stress fractures in his foot. They got so bad that he couldn't even stand up. While he ran I cleaned until the house smelt like bleach, like nothing, everywhere except Seth's room.

'Are you feeling any better?' I kneel beside him. He just snorts and shuffles onto his side, reaches for the beer. He winces as he takes a sip.

'How much longer are you going to do this for?' I ask, taking the bottle from him. 'You have to get out of bed eventually.'

'I know.' He looks up at me and for a few seconds I see the old Karl, the Karl with that full, thrilling laugh and a smile like a lit bulb; the Karl who wouldn't try to drink himself through this.

'Were there people here before?' he asks.

I want to show him the tooth, tell him that it's finally over, but instead I just kiss him on the head and hand him back the bottle.

'Don't worry about it, love. It was just more journalists asking about Seth.' He drains the rest of the beer, closes his eyes. By the time I reach the bedroom door it seems like he's already asleep.

*

Seth was an accident. Everyone else called him a miracle. He was born just before my forty-fifth birthday, though Karl and I had stopped trying to conceive years before that. I had restricted fallopian tubes, what one specialist referred to as lazy tubes. We used to joke that they were Catholic tubes, that God tied them in punishment for never tying the knot with Karl. Money was too tight for IVF and Karl didn't want to raise someone else's child, so adoption was out. We decided to make do and get on with our lives. When I stopped getting my period I thought that menopause had started early, but then I couldn't fit into my work uniform and I started craving bacon at all hours of the night.

He was six weeks premature, a knuckle of skin and hair in the incubator. His immune system was so weak I had to wear gloves and a surgical mask when I finally got to hold him. The doctors said it was unlikely he would ever reach a healthy weight, that there could be developmental delays. I nodded along as they spoke, but I wasn't really listening. I was praying to a god I didn't believe in that he would survive. Even if he was stuck in a wheelchair for the rest of his life, even if he couldn't speak to me, even if he didn't know who I was. I cupped his welt-red body in my hands and I prayed.

'Have you spoken to the police about the door?' Audrey unloads the shopping onto the kitchen table. Cans of soup and tinned peaches, a 10-kilogram bag of rice. Food for an apocalypse.

'Bloody animals. You shouldn't have to put up with that, you know.'

Audrey's been bringing us groceries to save me from showing my face in town. Her son Jackson was in Seth's year at school. We met judging the long jump at the boys' athletics day. I was a good ten years older than most of the other mothers, the only one with liver spots and crook wrists. Some of them mistook me for Mrs Hawkswell, the English teacher who was set to retire at the end of term. One of the mothers even stood in front of me and grilled me about her child's performance.

Audrey was the only one who bothered with me. We measured the jumps, chatting about our sons' teachers, their marks, what we wanted them to study at uni. Jackson was top of the class and dead set on engineering. I said that Seth was a whiz on computers, that he was passionate about current affairs. I didn't tell her that he'd put a padlock on his door, that he never seemed to sleep. I didn't tell her how worried I was.

While I jotted down the distances of the jumps on a clipboard, Seth was trudging round the track, headphones crammed over his long black hair. The other kids snickered as they bounded past. He clumped along, glaring at the ground, annihilating it with his eyes. I wanted to do something, to reach out, but I knew how it would look, the ancient mother with the daggy sunhat, trying to hug her son.

Now Audrey and I sit across from each other at the kitchen table, both of us looking down at our laps, waiting for the kettle to boil.

'How are you feeling?' Audrey says, gripping my hands in hers. I can smell rosewater on her wrists.

I've been asked that question so many times: by counsellors and by the journalists who were camped outside our house, by the police even. By Karl, by my second cousin on the phone. The truth is that I don't know. Dr Joyce says it's important to try to label my feelings, to give myself permission to grieve, but it seems dishonest to say that I'm feeling fine or bad or sad or empty or numb. Audrey's hands are still in mine and I have the mad idea to squeeze them, to squeeze them so hard that her fingers break, but I keep my eyes on the tabletop, use my bitten fingernails to pick at the divots that Seth used to score into the Formica with his knife and fork at dinnertime.

'Let's not talk about that,' I say in that voice which doesn't sound like mine. 'Tell me about Jackson.'

She gets up and tips the tea leaves into the pot, leaves it to steep. When she sits back down she's looking at me warily. 'Jacks is good. He got through all of his exams okay, but he said that Chemistry was tough. He's heading down to the Gold Coast for Schoolies and then he's going with his mates on a road trip. We're trying to get him back for Christmas because Paul's family is flying in from up north.' I swim in her voice, her easy, normal words. 'If you and Karl don't have any plans you're welcome to join us, it won't be anything fancy but —'

'He told us he was going to Schoolies,' I say. 'Seth did. A few months ago he said that he wanted to go with mates to Bali. We were just happy that he had friends, though we'd never met any of them. He seemed, I don't know, content since the start of this year. He'd cut his hair and the teachers said he'd started paying attention in class. Sometimes he'd even talk to me when he'd get home from school. He just seemed like he was getting better, like he was finally becoming a regular teenager.'

'But there's no such thing as a regular teenager,' Audrey says. 'You never know what they're thinking. Sometimes I'll try to talk to Jackson and he'll just stare right through me. Sometimes I think, "Who is this person?" How could you have known?'

'We bought him the passport. We bought it for him. It was supposed to be a reward if he passed all his exams, but he disappeared before, well, you know all that. The police think that the recruiters gave him the money for the ticket to Turkey.'

'You can't blame yourself. It could have happened to anybody.'

Audrey's nodding along as I talk, head cocked in concern. I imagine her getting home in an hour or so, popping her head into Jackson's room to make sure he's had something to eat. I imagine her getting him ready for his trip, making him promise to take plenty of photos, telling him to call her if he needs extra cash, feeling so thankful it wasn't her son. Momentarily I hate her, I want to throw her out, but I don't know whether I can bear sitting alone in the house, waiting for the phone to ring.

'You probably think there were times when Seth hurt animals or something like that,' I say. 'But I never noticed any anger in him. It just seemed like he was never really there. I don't know. Karl and I tried to get through to him, but maybe we were too old.'

At my last session Dr Joyce said I'm in control of my own story. I can choose to interpret this however I want to. It's my decision how I remember Seth, how I choose to think of him.

I walk over to the fridge, take the laminated newspaper clipping from under the magnet. I bring it over to Audrey. It's a photo of Karl and me standing at night in front of the fig tree down the side of the house. We're bathed in a milky light, from the white fairy lights wrapped around the tree's branches. The caption says, 'Karl and Clementine Kenny: the King and Queen of Christmas'.

'We won that silly competition that the local paper runs, you know the one, for best decorations.'

'Of course,' Audrey says.

I take the photo from her, hold it up to my face. Karl had come home from Bunnings one day, his car loaded with boxes of fairy lights. Dozens of them, all white.

'He said we were going to have a white Christmas.'

'Who did?' Audrey asks, confused.

Karl would get up on the roof in the mornings and sometimes in the late afternoon when it wasn't too hot, piling the lights into mounds so they looked like banks of snow. When he turned them on at night, it looked like we were in Europe in the middle of winter.

Seth, who was ten or eleven at the time, spent most of the summer holidays on the computer. One night, I heard him walk out of his bedroom and into the garden. I followed him down the side of the house, tiptoeing so he wouldn't hear me. He was standing under the branches of the fig tree, looking up into the light, as if in a trance.

'He looked so peaceful.' I put the photo down on the table.

'Who did? Seth? I can't see him in the photo.' Audrey sneaks a look at her watch. 'Well, Clem, it's getting la—'

'Wait. I'm trying to remember.'

When Seth finally noticed me standing there he smiled and said, 'I've never seen snow before.' We kept the lights up for months after that. Every night when it got dark we'd take our dinner plates and eat on a rug under the tree. Then there was a big storm and the cabling was wrecked. It took Karl a few days to get it working again, and the next time we took Seth out to look he said that the light hurt his eyes.

Audrey doesn't have any idea what I'm talking about, but I'm seeing things clearly for the first time, I'm seeing that this is the Seth that I should choose to remember.

'They think they've found his body,' I say. I'm speaking so quietly I can't hear myself over the rain. I say it again. 'A bomb blast in a shopping centre. They came this morning for his teeth.'

Maybe I didn't say anything, because Audrey is yawning and standing up from the table. 'I better get going, Clem, before it starts hailing.'

She pauses for a moment to see if I'm going to say anything, then disappears down the hall. I feel the storm building in my ankles and wrists, the way it always does since my arthritis got worse. How could I feel the weather changing, in my own body, but I didn't pick up the change in him? Feeling tired, I get up from the table and walk to the back of the house. I haven't been in his room since the police came for his things, but I lie on his bed. The glow-in-the-dark stars on Seth's ceiling are dimmer now, but I can still make them out. I count a couple of dozen before they all blur together.

*

I can hear Audrey's footfalls coming down the hallway. She's knocking at the door, pushing it open.

'There are people outside. Where's Karl?' Audrey starts shaking me. 'Clem. Clem. Get out here quick.'

Light's shining through the frosted glass panels on the sides of the front door. We rush into the living room, peek through the curtains. The sky's still dark but our front lawn's lit up, the grass soupy with mud. The sound of an engine over the rain. I see the outline of a ute and a spotlight on top of the cab shining into the house. Figures jump down from the tray, walk through the front gate. They're wearing hoodies and sunglasses and they're carrying golf clubs.

There are thumps on the front door, on the roof, on the outside of the house. Audrey grips my hand like Seth used to when he was young. Something smashes through the window beside us and lands on the coffee table. There are cackles of laughter. I see a smear of red on the broken windowpane. The next one lands on Audrey's sandals. It's a cane toad, with a hole in its side from where the golf club went in. Its heart ripples in its chest as it bleeds over Audrey's toes.

'Bastards. Call the police, Clem,' shouts Audrey as she runs for the front door, flecks of glass flying from her hair. I follow in slow motion to the threshold of the door. Outside I can see two figures waiting by the birdbath with buckets in their hands.

'That's the mother.' I recognise his voice from the night before. One of them trips Audrey as she runs past and she skids into the grass. They hoist up the buckets and dump the cane toads over her. They roar like they're at a football game, as the toads writhe and skip across her hair her face her chest.

'Not on our fucking watch, you terrorist bitch,' one of them jeers.

I can't move from the doorway. I should be running for the phone, or to help my friend, but I just stand here and take Seth's tooth from my bra, squeeze it as hard as I can.

Seth found the teeth the day before he left. I kept them in a Milo tin at the back of the pantry. When I came home from work he was sitting at the kitchen table in his school uniform, looking disgruntled, the teeth arranged in front of him.

'I've been saving them.' I smiled and put my hand on his shoulder.

'But why do you have them?' He stared at me blankly.

'Because they're a part of you.'

'That's fucked up.' He wrenched my hand away, scattering the teeth on the floor. He stared at me from his chair while I crawled across the tiles, counted the teeth back into the tin. Maybe that's how I should remember him instead, staring down at me with those blank blue eyes. Maybe this will help me harden my heart.

*

'Mum?'

The spotlight shuts off and someone jumps down from the cab of the ute, runs over and crouches beside Audrey. The rain's so heavy it takes me a moment to recognise Jackson, her son, the captain of the rugby team, with his long lean arms and pink cheeks. Frantic, he flicks toads off her, hugs her close to him. He helps her up and ushers her into the ute. The others stand around as if deciding what to do.

'Come on. Let's get the fuck out of here.' Jackson calls from the driver's seat. They climb in and the ute careens down the street, flicking mud behind it.

I still haven't moved. I watch the Christmas lights glowing on our neighbour's roof as they drive away, glance down at my hand. A runnel of blood is trickling down the middle of my palm, from where the tip of Seth's tooth has pierced the skin.

He swallowed one when he was nine years old. He shook me awake in the middle of the night and told me in a breathless, lisping whisper that he thought the tooth would grow in his tummy, that it would eat him up from the inside. I was just so glad he was telling me what was wrong. I took him into the kitchen and made him a cup of Metamucil. We played Battleship until he could go to the toilet. I reminded him to wipe. I told him that in a few days the tooth would be gone and that seemed to calm him down. I took him back to bed and we counted the glow-in-the-dark stars on his ceiling until he fell asleep.

*

The phone starts to ring in the hall. I walk in from the verandah, stand in front of the cradle. I don't pick it up. Instead I take Seth's baby tooth, the last part of him that hasn't been taken from me, and place it in my mouth. I remember when Seth woke me that night, I remember his wild white face swimming in the dark. This is how I choose to remember him. At first the tooth settles in my throat, but after a few swallows I get it down. I rip the phone's cord out of the socket.

Karl's stirring in the bed when I get in beside him, put my head on his chest. He's slept through this whole night, it seems like he's slept through all of it. I can smell beer and sweaty skin under his leg brace, but I nestle in as close as I can.

'I thought I heard Seth before?' he says, still half-asleep. 'Is everything all right?'

The hailstones sound like teeth chattering on the roof and we lie there, thinking of him, side by side in the eye of the storm.

The Encyclopaedia of Wild Things

Madeline Bailey

Fox.

In Year 4 we built a fox. We made it out of facts, so it was bigger than a real fox, and slinkier. It prowled between the bushes in the scrubland behind the oval. We pretended to play cricket, but we were watching the shrubs swish. We lost score each time we thought we heard it padding.

Somebody said the fox was red like jam – except its tail and its paw-tips, which were milky. Tim was my best friend, he said the fox loved eating children (chewy hats). He said the only taste she loved more was shortbread. This meant that if you fed her all the biscuits from your lunch box you could pass. These were good facts.

I said all this explained why Callum hadn't been in class: Callum never shared his shortbread. When the fox found out she ate him. Everyone agreed that this was also a good fact, because in Year 4 no one knew Callum had cancer.

All of us built the fox but it went wild. It kept soaking up stories, so we couldn't stop it growing and we had to make a plan to protect parents. We never told about the fox because we didn't want to scare them. We just said school rules had changed and now they always had to wait in the top car park – which was concrete, with no shrubs.

Space.

My dad was good at reading and he knew a lot of stories. Sometimes he brought his volumes of *Encyclopaedia Britannica* to read to me and scanned them for the good bits about stars. Stars can look faint from the Earth but still be bright, you just can't tell 'cause there is interstellar dust. I like space. I like how space is never stable, it is relative (relies on your perspective).

Sometimes my dad brought newspapers. He read me sections about politics and culture, also travel. I watched his mouth move through the gaps. The newspapers were gappy 'cause my dad tore out the sections that had smashed cars or pictures of wars. I knew because I found them in the bin and read them all. I wished I hadn't.

My dad was good at reading. He was also good at fixing. He bought my backpack from an op shop but he fixed it: he stitched stars on. While I was at school he fixed the house, he hand-washed dishes and he ironed all the crushed parts out of clothes. When we got home he fixed us toast. He burnt it often but I didn't mind (we added butter).

Dad fixed our sink, our car, our gutters – and my rocket, when I dropped it. He glued the fins back on and they stopped being cracked and wonky. After it was saved, it was shinier. It glinted like my dad's earrings, and his polished leather boots.

Weather.

My dad never forgot the stuff I'd told him. This meant that when the bell rang he would be in the top carpark, with a cluster of the mothers. All the mothers loved my dad, he gave them novels to borrow, knew good facts, brought spare umbrellas on damp days to make sure no-one else's windcheaters went soggy.

I would linger in the cloakroom so he'd have time to talk to other people. Sometimes he had too many facts. He had nobody he could tell.

I wished that I was good at fixing, but I was not good at much. Out of my class I was the worst at spelling. On Tuesdays we had tests and it was often the same words. I still forgot them. I thought perhaps their letters could have shifted round since last week.

We had to write the plural word for woman. I wrote *whimen* (it's a shifty word, sounds like it might be open to an *h*).

The teacher said: *No, George, you cannot keep the extra letters.* She said I had to read more, to remember better English.

I would read an awful lot. I'd read *Britannica* whenever I was worried. *Britannica* said foxes are land mammals with large natural distributions and in Greek myth one got turned into a star. It also said about the foxtrot, foxglove flowers, and Fox Films. Words slipped into other words: the more I read, the worse I'd spell.

Silver.
I did not like Callum much. He always wore these silver sneakers. They were crinkly like space boots – and they flashed.

In Year 4 my sneakers were beige and too big (stupid op shop). I did not like Callum much. He was too lucky.

Fire.
Tim was my best friend. I did not like him much either but I liked visiting his house. His mum baked cupcakes and they came out of the oven spongy, round, in silver trays. We ate them in Tim's lounge room, by the fire. It had no matches or logs because it came with a remote. Tim pressed the rubber buttons then the flames went blue or bigger. Tim said his father bought it because charcoal stains the carpet.

Tim's house had an upstairs but it was only for adults. Tim said he had snuck up once and the rooms had plusher couches. His father invited guests there so upstairs had to stay clean. Guests meant work friends, and some of the other mothers, who would all be offered coffee and asked to chat for a bit. But when he came to pick me up, guests did not seem to mean my dad.

Fish.
The pot plant on our deck was dead, but Dad watered it just in case.

When we went to the hardware store I waited outside, near the pond, and counted all the coins that people had tossed to the bottom. It was hard to see sometimes 'cause there were fish there, who I hated.

Dad bought tinned paint or rope, then gave me change to make a wish. I wished the pot plant on our deck would please un-die, but it did not. When we got home it was still wilty and I knew Dad's change was wasted.

At the hardware store, the next time, there were no coins in the pond. The fish were bigger. I knew they'd eaten my wishes.

Trains.

Tim said a group of mothers from our class would meet for picnics every Sunday, and that each one brought a tub of their home-cooking. Tim said you could cram chunks of all the best cakes in your pockets, then go play.

All the mothers loved my dad, except he never got invited to these picnics.

I still dreamt them. I imagined they were in the park with the train playground. My entire class was there and all the mothers flitted round placing a rug, opening tubs. They had brought cupcakes. Also cookies, muffins, scones and all the other special things that you can bake in silver trays.

But my dad has no trays like that. He brought burnt toast. And when the picnic got packed up, all of the plastic tubs were empty except his, which no-one wanted. So Dad took the toast home cold as it was bad toast, square and wrong and my dad brought the spare umbrellas, but *No, George, no extra letters.*

Facts fold into other facts.

Seagulls.

Once Tim asked me: *George, what is your dad?*

That lunchtime he had played badly in cricket. I'd played worse – but it never seemed to matter.

I said my dad was the best reader, the best fixer; he was also the best sailor. I had not watched him sail but I knew that he was good 'cause of the trophies. There were lots tucked in his wardrobe. They were topped with metal ships. The gold paint was a bit scuffed but they still meant my dad had sailed and he'd won a lot of races. But Dad said that what with one thing and another you stop sailing – you're doing other things, but that's okay.

Sometimes, if Dad looked tired, I would ask him for a good fact about ships. Dad glowed when he talked about ships. I learned that while you're racing you read weather by watching the seagulls tilt like metal windvanes. I learned Dad built his first boat and it was a racing dinghy – it had sails on each side, they were called wings. Dad said they were made of canvas but I still pictured them feathered.

I told Tim all of this that time he asked: *What is your dad?*

He didn't listen. He said: *Your dad is a fag.*

Shoes.

In Year 5 we get a notice about Callum. We have to give the notice to our parents so that they will know the news. The news we got told in the morning. The notice also says there'll be a service at the school and a support plan for the students who are grieving.

I read *Britannica* as soon as I get home. I look up *shoes*. Shoes are part of fashion but also of archaeology, and horseshoes have been thought to hold good luck.

You would think that silver sneakers would hold good luck in them, too.

Words.

On Mondays, now, I see a man. He has an office near my classroom with two chairs, also some crayons in a mug. On his door there is a photo full of cows.

I think he saw me count them our first Monday 'cause he said: *They're highland cattle.* He said they are a joke, because he's Scottish.

Today the man says I should tell him what I'm thinking. I could tell him words are wild, but I do not want to scare him. So instead I lie and say I'm thinking how I'm still the worst at spelling.

The man nods (crinkled forehead) then he asks: *Do you feel perilous?*

I do not understand what he means by *perilous*. It's an odd word, it just makes me think of spacemen. I guess *perilous* could sound like a good word about exploring: a good word for muddling boundaries, shuffling rules?

I had felt *perilous* the day we got that notice for our parents, 'cause I did not give the notice to my dad. I tore it up. Then chewed the pieces. So you could not read the print. Not even if you found them in the bin. That night Dad asked me *George, how was your day?* and I said *Fine* and then I asked him for a good fact about ships.

I picture Dad tucked in a boat with feathered wings. Inside it smells like buttered toast. He's fixing sails, reading weather – wearing polished pirate boots – and even though it makes no sense it is the bravest, brightest boat, and so if anyone is *perilous* it's Dad.

Then I remember that the man is Scottish. And he has a Scottish voice. And so he had wanted a different word, he just couldn't pronounce it.

He had meant to ask: Do you feel *powerless*?

The Boat

Joshua Mostafa

His name is Paul or Peter, I forget. We sit together, squashed among a couple dozen others like the human luggage that we are, below the deck, where years of putrefying fish have left their stink. No windows. Someone's puked. An infant cries.

I fold my arms and try to think of nothing, but he's talking in my ear again. About a boat, not this one, not the filthy bucket that we're crammed inside; a sailboat, one he used to own, his pride and joy, it seems – though he insists it's not a yacht. The word's incongruous, as if it's from another language, moulded by the habits of a foreign and exotic world. I try it on my tongue, repeating: yacht. A laugh begins to bubble up, or is it just a retch, the air is hot and thick.

He won't stop talking, god knows why he thinks he's found a kindred spirit, maybe just because I'm softly spoken, or that when he said that this last fortnight, crammed inside a fishy tin, had spoiled his love of seafood, I agreed, and when he rhapsodised about a little place in Darlinghurst that used to serve the most delicious oyster bisque, I said I used to eat there too. And now, despite the fact that Darlinghurst is just another wasteland – gutted houses, burned-out cars, a battleground for warring gangs, where feral dogs and beggar children prowl for scraps – it lives in both our memories, the strolls we individually took, a coffee on a Sunday afternoon, an exhibition opening. He seems delighted by this reminiscence, puckering his flabby lips as if it brings him closer to the life he's lost. Our country. Just a dream, a make-believe. I don't know when it ceased to be, but it was well before I paid my passage at the dock: 'No Aussie dollars! Euros, yuan, American or gold' (I gave the smugglers all I had: my ring, my granddad's watch). Perhaps it stopped existing when the riots started, tearing through the CBD. Perhaps it faltered in the drought, and dried up with the dying crops, and hollowed out as shops and supermarkets closed their doors. Perhaps when all the television channels flickered out, and then the power stopped. That global warming nonsense, Peter says (or Paul), the Chinese wouldn't buy our coal – they caught a cold, we sneezed – a perfect storm. I envy him a little: even now, when everything's collapsed, his stock of simple clichéd explanations is intact. Like all the men, our beards are growing wild – no razors anymore – but he, I reckon, must have had a pale moustache, a perfect barrier that filtered any doubts or contradictory thoughts as he inhaled. But maybe not. There's something in his eyes. A trembling of the iris, creature-panic that he can't conceal, for all his talk. He flinches when the hatch is opened, sunlight streaming in, but it is just our daily meal.

The smuggler bringing us our food descends the rungs and pauses, screwing up his face, disgusted by our stench and, when he sees our eager hands outstretched to take the meagre rations, laughs and taunts us in his language, holds the first container out of reach, and toys with us, enjoying his contempt. I'm not too proud to beg – I lift my arms and wait until he's bored of tantalising us and hands the plastic boxes out. It's rice, again – the grains are hard (half-undercooked, half-burnt) and indistinguishable puréed vegetables whose blandness is enlivened by the tang of slight decay. I'm hungry, though. I force down every scrap.

My neighbour on the other side refuses his; instead, he takes a strip of jerky from the stash inside his jacket and begins to chew it with his bony jaws. Can't stand that Asian crap, he says, his nostrils flaring as he eyes my rancid meal. His weathered skin is lizard-like, a mass of blotchy freckles, taut across his bones. With spindly fingers he withdraws a few tobacco threads and rolls a tiny smoke. I'd go a parmy, he says meditatively, you reckon they have pubs in Indo, probably fucking not, shariah law. But where you're from – the Middle East, wherever – what's the go there:

can you get a drink? I tell him I'm from Erskineville; he's obviously sceptical, but lets it pass. He asks the smuggler, how much longer on the boat, you said a week, you lying cunts. The smuggler isn't listening; a shout above has made him stiffen in alarm. The mocking smile is gone, he glares around at us and puts a finger to his lips. He leaves the last containers in a heap and climbs the ladder, slamming tight the hatch. A frantic, hungry scrabble for the boxes. A young and hefty man – from Tonga, maybe – breaks it up, and passes out the food. The very last container goes to Paul (or Peter), who is unimpressed – a bloody outrage, are they trying to kill us – but he eats his portion anyway, his blunt and pallid paws delivering each morsel to his plump and ginger-whiskered mouth. That fleshy head. A walrus, like the song. And all at once I want to get away. But if I stand, I'm sure I'll spew, and I'm too weak to lose today's allotted meal. I'll bide my time until the nausea's passed. And then I'll stumble to the other side and sit between that Tongan lad and some old woman who has been asleep for hours – that'll be a better spot than sitting here between the lizard man and Paul.

He's droning on; I've mentioned, foolishly, I used to play the violin, and now he's telling me about the time he went to see an opera – *Carmen*, something shit. I try to be as blunt as possible: I don't like Bizet, and the Opera House is just an empty shell, there's nothing there. But Peter doesn't seem to understand. It's such a tragedy, he says, and launches into yet another elegy to leisures lost: to single malts, to wagyu beef, to dinner parties, wine and cheese; to golf, to watching cricket on a Sunday afternoon; to nights at the casino, getaways in the Barossa, harbour sailing in his boat that's not a yacht. I cannot bring myself to say shut up. Politeness has no purpose in this world, as utterly redundant as his cultivated tastes, but I can't shake it off. If I can take one shred of bitter satisfaction from the chaos that's engulfed my country, killed so many thousands, scattered friends, destroyed my home, it's this: the likes of Paul, the status-conscious, vain, self-satisfied, adept at office politics and purchasing investment properties, a little poison now and then for pleasant dreams, this species, *homo mediocris*, isn't – after all – the last of men. There are no crafty, well-timed deals to strike, no stocks and shares, conspicuous consumption, status signals, subtle as a horse turd steaming on a lawn – they don't exist. And yet in any conversation he returns to them, like some old fool repeating senile stories, stoking feebly at the embers of the glories of his youth. I almost pity him, undignified and obsolete, unkempt, a dirty crumpled suit, anonymous, another in the mass of human maggots wriggling out the orifices of the national corpse. And even here, as cargo in a smuggler's hold, the only way he can communicate is with his repertoire of boasts and humblebrags: the brand of car he used to drive (before the petrol pumps were seized for the exclusive use of this or that militia's vehicles), the house he used to live in (waterfront – he wouldn't call it absolute, not quite) and then, most casually of all, the boat that's not a yacht, but which, no doubt, if I could see it, would impress me with its yacht-like qualities; its almost-yachtishness would validate his understated taste – as well, of course, as wealth with which to use it – not to mention the exquisite modesty he shows by claiming that it wasn't quite a yacht.

The gaunt man with the lizard skin, who's sat in silence listening and chewing on his strand of jerky, coughs a gob of brown saliva on the floor before our feet. Aw, yeah? You going fucking sailing, cunt? Wank on. The only boat for you is with the rest of us, in this old piece of shit. Your precious boat is gone, cunt: bloody gone. Some arsehole might have sunk it just for shits and giggles – if it's still afloat, some eastside mob has got it, bet you anything your fucking yacht is full of little soft-cock Jew-boys, leather jackets, think they're gangsters, showing off for Bondi bimbo whores. The lizard-man lets out a wheezing laugh. He's odious in every way, but I can't help but chuckle at the face that Paul makes, mottled outrage, ruddy with affront. He splutters out an angry word or two.

From elsewhere, suddenly, a deep but startled cry booms out and echoes round the hold. The Tongan guy is staring, horrified: the woman who's been still for hours at a stretch has pitched facedown upon the floor. My God, says Peter, is she dead? – she's dead! For fuck's sake, says the thin man, she's been dead since yesterday, and none of youse cunts knew? The shock has made us all – well, all but me – forget to keep our voices down, but even through the din of shouting I can hear a thud of footsteps on the deck above. I try to hush my fellow passengers. It's hopeless, they're oblivious. More steps. I think I know, or fear, who it must be. I find I'm screaming: never mind the dead! We're still alive! And they can find us here!

A sudden silence. All eyes on the hatch. It jolts, and creaks, and opens, slowly, and as if my words have brought him into being, there he is, a soldier, sailor, coastguard or police, it doesn't matter: haloed by the sun, a man in uniform. He stares down at us, at our filthy faces, slumped together in this squalid hold, a smudge or smear of humankind that might have once played violin, or sailed a pretty boat that wasn't quite a yacht; so what? He speaks some language we don't need to understand: his eyes, triumphant, speak for him. It's over now, they say. Your boat's been stopped.

Glisk

Josephine Rowe

We are wading out, the five of us. I remember this. The sun an hour or two from melting into the ocean, the slick trail of its gold showing the way we will take.

Ahead of me, my tiny sister sits regal and unafraid in the middle of the raft that Fynn has built from packing foam and empty chemical buckets, lids fixed airtight with caulk. He's already tested it out in our neighbours' pool and declared it seaworthy, but if the thing falls apart he has promised to carry Sara himself. Fynn is thirteen, older than me by five years, and the only one of us three kids who has been to the island before. Our mother had long hair then, and Fynn's dad was still around, hadn't yet skidded his motorbike underneath a roadtrain. My dad – Fynn's dad too now, Mum constantly reminds us – shoulders a picnic basket filled with Sara's favourites, Fynn's favourites, Mum's favourites, mine: cheese and apple sandwiches, salt and vinegar chips, slivers of mango doused with lime and chilli, ginger beer. Enough food to last a week, though we'll be crossing back to the mainland this same night, lit by a quarter moon and a two-dollar torch.

The people around us hardly seem like people. More like a muster of herd animals. They move steadily through the water in ones and twos, feeling for the slope of the sandbar underfoot, the treacherous edge where the ocean floor falls away. That's how people – tourists, mostly – get themselves drowned, snatched off by rips.

The sea the sea the terrible ...

Yep yep, we say, we know; Dad gets wordy sometimes.

There are other families, some also towing small children on boogie boards, inflatable lilos, nothing so fine as Sara's raft. Eskies bob alongside silver jellyfish-balloons of clothes tied inside plastic shopping bags.

We're lucky, Dad's telling us, today's a neap tide – safest time to make a crossing. The highest tide not as high as normal, the deepest part not so deep.

Further out, the island looks like a rough dog slouching up from the ocean, muzzle pointed north-west. What's out there? A lot of putrid birds, Fynn's already told me, and some all right caves, mobs of bogans sinking tinnies. Nothing awesome. But tonight, after sunset, the shores around the island will be phosphorescent with the visiting swarm of bio-luminescent phytoplankton, on their anxious, brilliant way to who-knows-where. We'll perch along the highest bluff in a sprawl of blankets and eskies while the waves crash iridescent against the rocks below, sweeping back to leave lonely blue stars stranded here and there, then charging back in to reclaim them.

It will be spectacular, an eerie sort of magic, and I will never see anything like it again.

But whatever, this isn't the point. In the end, the island is just a dog-shaped rock covered with birds and sunburnt gawkers, temporarily surrounded by terrified dinoflagellates.

It's this wading out that matters, this crossing: the bright, migratory-animalness of it. Going waist deep, chest deep, waist deep again.

What matters is how, halfway over, Fynn looks back at us, then ahead again, and says to no one, or everyone, or maybe just to Sara:

I reckon this is how the afterlife must look.

I see Dad look back at Mum and mouth the word, *afterlife?*

Fynn is the palest of us, lighter even than Mum; blonde right to his eyelashes, the only one who crisps up in the sun. He looks adopted. A thing we all know but know better than to say.

Anyway. There it is.

Do I make it through childhood without staking every possible biological claim on the man who calls us both *my beloved savage*? I'm ashamed to say I do not. I'm content to share him only in his lesser moments: it is my dad who used to play bass in an almost-famous blues band, but it is our dad who, before the blues band, used to play clarinet in a high school orchestra. It is my dad who promises to buy us a pair of albino axolotls, our dad who reneges when Fynn and I neglect our goldfish duties and Skeletor's tank is all slime and fug.

(There was a time, some years, where it was just Fynn and Mum, and this is maybe what I'm getting back at him for. Or else I'm getting him back for all the names he isn't called in school, the way no one ever asks where he's from, whether his parents are *reffos*. Or else it's the fact that, even though one of them is dead, he has two fathers, doesn't have to share his, and is allowed to wander off without telling anyone, to give reasons like 'just thinking' or 'just walking', getting soft looks instead of strife.)

Does my brother find some spiteful way of getting even, of undermining my full-bloodedness? He never does. Maybe he never feels the need to. Fynn takes these pissing contests for what they are. In actual pissing contests, there is no competition, and really no point. He gets halfway to the bougainvillea tumbling over the top of the fence, while I try (no hands) not to dribble on my runners.

*

At the deepest point of the crossing, the ocean reaches my lower lip, and I hold onto Mum. Feel my feet levitate from the shell grit below. Become cargo swinging from her strong gold shoulder, safe in her smell of coconut oil and warm bread as she pushes on towards the island.

Around us the ocean thickens to an algaeic soup that stinks of dead things; proof that the plankton are here, all around us, though invisible for now – it isn't dark enough to give them away yet. This is the point where Fynn's raft begins to keel, the empty buckets unhitching, and Sara responds with a lot of high-pitched wailing and clutching at salty air.

When the raft breaks apart, Fynn keeps his word, and Sara scrambles up from the wreckage to ride his bony shoulders, her little grabby starfish hands clenching fistfuls of his tawny hair. It must hurt badly, his eyes pulled to teary slits, but he says nothing while trying to shepherd pieces of the debris ahead of himself.

Waves slap at his face, trying to get in through his mouth and nose. He screws his eyes shut, snorts water, while higher up Sara sings, oblivious, her stubby little feet hooked under his wrists.

Hey mate, Dad offers, I can take her. But both Fynn and Sara shake their heads, so Dad just cruises alongside in a coastguard sort of way, until the ocean finally slips from Fynn's shoulders and leaves Sara cheerily marooned up there.

There are no photographs from that day. Mum dropped the disposable QuickSnap crossing back to the mainland, and though we groped and kicked around no one found it. Perhaps that's why I remember it so vividly. Fynn stumbling through the breakers with Sara, delivering her safely to the dry sand and waiting until Mum had led her off to squeak into some penguin burrows before he doubled over and gushed out all that swallowed seawater into a patch of saltbrush. Fiery stinger marks striped his quaky legs.

Years later, somewhere into adulthood, I'll decide that this is a story to one day tell at my brother's wedding. Or else his funeral. Possibly both – as with a certain kind of suit, it seems workable for either occasion.

Instead of the wedding and/or funeral speech (though sure, there's still time enough for both), I'm delivering this story to my wife. Trying to wrest my brother back from what local mythology has made of him. Careless Idiot at best; Murderer at worst. Ti has been driving past those crosses at the shoulder of Highridge Road for years, since before we even met. Shed-made, white as desert-bleached bones.

Coated with a fresh layer of paint every spring, strung with teddy bears, ribbons, other sentimental lark. Trinkets refreshed each September, along with the paint. The grandparents' work, we suspect; the father too modest for that sort of rubbish.

This is all Ti knows of my brother. This, and the couple-three cards he's sent, and the shedful of furniture he left behind; all gliding teak curves and high-tension wires. *Mid-century harpsichord*, Ti calls it, explaining how *their* father was a luthier when friends admire the coffee table, the only piece that makes sense with the rest of our house.

My father, I'll sometimes add. My father was the luthier.

Why, Ti wants to know, would your brother come back here?

I ask myself the same.

After the hearing, depending on who you care to ask, Fynn either *ran, slunk, snuck, crawled, choofed-off, fucked-off, hauled arse*, or simply *went* to the Northern Isles of Scotland, where the Atlantic rushes in to meet the North Sea, and where he got some shit-kicking work at a whisky distillery. There he works five or six shifts a week, making nothing that anyone could put his name to.

I still draw sometimes, he told me once, glitchy at his end of our sole Skype attempt. His face freezing then catching up with itself.

I still sketch out ideas for things I might make one day if I ever [garble].

Last year Mum and Dad retired to Norfolk Island. Mum phones every Sunday to talk politics and weather and to ask what the hell she did wrong. Sara is twenty-five, working as an image and style consultant in Sydney. Who knows what she thinks; she's less scrutable than a butchy boy. She doesn't remember that trip to the island, or the raft, and I'm not sure she remembers a time when she liked either of us, Fynn or me. Her first memories start at five, and by then Fynn was sixteen, flakey as a box of Frosties, and I was a monster. Long gone are the days when she would laugh along with whatever jokes we told, not understanding but not wanting to be left out. Sometimes we would laugh just to make her laugh, tell jokes that weren't funny, or weren't even real jokes but had the rhythm of jokes. Just to test her, just to watch her go. Now she doesn't find anything funny.

I think you ruined her, Mum says down the phone one weekend. You and your brother.

When did he become mine is a question I do not ask.

Fynn arrives on a Saturday morning with one duffel bag, his blondness gone to seed, hair brushing the collar of the bomber jacket he wears in spite of the January heat. Dead pine trees still line the curb, flung out for green waste.

My brother lopes across the scorched front lawn, looking even older than he looked in court, older than I figured possible. Walking taller than he wants to be, ghosting up the morning. Out on the street there's his rental hatchback, some hairdryer, crouching as though it also hopes not to be seen. As though six years might be too soon.

I'm waiting behind the flyscreen, feeling everything I'd neatly flat-packed springing up in me. I will punch him, I think. No, I will bring him in close. I will tell him ... I don't know what.

Yes, I might have picked him up from the airport, travelled that 80 k's with him – school doesn't start back till February, the course is all set, no one needs a thing from me till then. But I was thinking, stuff it. After this long and this much silence he can manage at least that much.

He's turning silver grey at the temples, and when he finally looks up his blue eyes waver as though he is looking at something unstill. He reminds me of those huskies that people, out of vanity or stupidity, see fit to keep as pets in this climate. Ti's hands ball into little fists when she sees them: bewildered, patchy-coated animals paraded around Perth's richer suburbs, humiliated wolves.

Fynn is humiliated, of course. He is beyond humiliated.

Hey! I say. Then, like an idiot, Welcome back!

Raf, is all he says, putting his hand forward like I'm about to go and shake it.

I step out into the glare and grab him around the shoulders, and he stands there stiffly for a few seconds, finally relenting to the hug.

Still in the doorway he rummages through the duffle bag. Brought you a gift, he says, but he says it like *geft*, this new lilt in his voice. Your wedding, he says, handing over a fancy wooden booze box.

Sorry I missed ... Then he waves a hand to mean: everything.

It strikes me that this is what strangers do. Make offerings before stepping over the thresholds of each other's houses. That this is what we are now.

Get in here, would you?

Inside he shucks off the bomber jacket. His skin is the bluish-white of those axolotls Dad never bought us.

Six summers, he explains, like an apology. A lot to make up for – mind if I go photosynthesise? Then he spends the next few hours just lying in our backyard, stripped down to his undies. Ti will be at work a few hours yet, dislodging pieces of Lego from the throats of small, stupid dogs, treating pissed-off cats for gingivitis. Fynn keeps his eyes closed as we speak about nothing much: Mum and Sara synching up their mid- and quarter-life crises; the Perth mining boom; the resulting ice boom; the inevitable rehab boom.

I rant about my students, mostly write-offs. Teaching them the difference between Rhizaria and Chromalveolata when it would be more use teaching them the difference between papillomavirus and chlamydia.

All the while my brother's face is turned directly towards the sun. I study the frail red and grey blood vessels on his near-translucent eyelids, limpid as rock-pool creatures down there in the deep set of his skull. The drive from the airport would have taken him past those crosses, the gleaming reinforced barrier.

What? he says from behind his closed eyes.

Nothing. You're burning, you know.

Beaut. Fine by me. Six bloody summers ...

Yeah yeah.

My wife falls in love with him, of course. Not in any way that could really be considered dangerous, just in the way I knew she would, the way people have always fallen in love with Fynn: quickly and easily and faithfully. *It is so so so good to finally finally meet you*, like a record jumping, and suddenly the crosses planted at the shoulder of the highway do not stand for two tiny girls and their singing-teacher mother. They stand for small-town intolerance, grudges borne longer than is fair or necessary, nourished by the kind of rural oxygen a larger city would have starved them of.

The two of them stand at the kitchen sink, elbow to elbow, de-bearding mussels. Cracking up over something I don't catch. In high school the couple of girls I managed to bring home laughed just as easily for him, like they were trying to wake up some sleeping thing. Fynn, my older, whiter brother, who never felt the need to take me down a notch. Who's always had everything going for him. Why do I still think of him this way? And why is there a moment, a flash in which I also think, *skulked, snuck, hauled-arse* ... after all the defending I've done in the years since the accident. Especially in the first couple, with people shaking their heads in the tinned fruit-and-veg aisle. Murmuring behind their hands at the cricket though all I have in common with Fynn is some blood.

I'm watching them over the top of my beer, my brother and my wife, somehow knowing, before it happens, that one of them is going to slice the paring knife through their palm, and the other is going to have an excuse to come at them with Dettol and cotton wool, and that I'm going to have to sit here and watch this. Then Fynn goes *Ah Christ!* but the gouge isn't deep, doesn't need Ti's attention, and he gets on with the job of scraping away the hairy tendrils that once anchored the mollusc someplace it thought sturdy.

Soon enough we're sitting around the table, butterflying shells between our fingers and using the halves for slurping up the briny liquor, the house filling with a fragrant, kelpy smell.

Ti has a theory about labour-intensive food, the kind where utensils are a waste of time and attempts at grace just make you clumsier. This theory holds: the empty shells pile up between us and the talk spills easily, as if we've been doing this every Saturday for years, the three of us.

The work's mostly just menial stuff, Fynn says. Bottling, label-ling. Keeping the mice off the malt floor. Things I can't mess up too bad. No hand in the art of it. But it's enough to be in that landscape – that old, that immense. Part of you just disappears.

All of you just disappeared, I think.

Got a little boat, he's saying. Take it out for sea trout on my days off. Bay of Isbister, Inganess ...

When he says these names it's with that lilt, as though the words have been kept in the wrappers they came in.

We drink all the wine that wasn't used to steam open the mussels, and when that's done we crack Fynn's wedding present. I uncork the heavy-based bottle, and the North Sea rushes into the room. I slosh out three glasses and we lift them to the wedding. We lift the next round to Dad's bypass, then another to the cousin whose dive gear let him down, and all the things that Fynn shouldn't have missed but did and oh well what can you do he's here now, hey?

Ti's giving me that *watch it* look; Fynn clears his throat and unfoots a mussel with a twist of fork, then goes back to seducing her with northernmost Scotland's beauty and gloom. The peat slabs cut and lifted out of the ground, snaked-through with heather roots and reeking of time. The salt air and natural violence that make their way into the bottle. The ocean and how it differs, how the memory of Western Australia shrinks right down to a pinhole. Standing at the edge of the Yesnaby Cliffs, clouds of guillemots beating frantic overhead.

Like the very ends of the earth out there, Fynn says.

Like the afterlife ...? And I can tell from how he looks at me that he doesn't remember ever saying that, that he thinks I'm taking the piss. None of us are quite drunk enough to not be embarrassed by this, so I refill our glasses and we drink to our sister, whose sense of humour we incrementally destroyed.

The bottle makes seven or eight rounds of our glasses before it's drained, and by that stage Ti has tapped out, her sturdy brown legs drawn up beneath her on the couch, her dark hair curtaining her from our nonsense.

Without her voice to anchor us there comes a drift, a silence so big and awful that it could be holding anything, but I know what's lurking. I try to head it off with small talk, but Fynn just nods. Here it comes, I think. Here it is.

You've seen him around, I s'pose?

Who?

Fynn shakes his head, as if I'm the coward.

Yeah. I see him sometimes. Not all that often.

And?

Look. Fynn. There's nothing I can tell you that's going to make you feel less shitful about it. Last year I saw him at the Farmers' Arms, and he looked like a man whose wife and kids had died five years ago. A few months back I saw him at the post office, and he looked like a man whose wife and kids had died six years ago. What else is there to say?

It happened in a heartbeat. In a *glisk*, Fynn has since said. Swerving to miss the dog that came trotting out of the scrub. Swinging his ute into the oncoming lane, into the oncoming sedan. Just a glisk, then. And the safety barrier just for show, apparently, eaten through by salt air and melting away like bad magic at the first kiss of fender.

I met a woman, Fynn says. Sweet clever type from the library. When I'd stay with her overnight, there'd be the sound of her kids running around the house in the morning. Sound of them laughing downstairs or talking in funny voices to the cat. It was too much, Raf. I couldn't tell her. And I couldn't stay.

I keep looking for something, my brother goes on. Something that'll fill up this scooped-out place but drink doesn't do it. Sex doesn't do it. I walk a bleeding lot, and the wind there wants to rip you open, but it isn't enough. I'll think maybe I can lose it in a roomful of people, like it'll be made to seem smaller somehow, but no, it's like everyone can all already see it, smell it on me.

I make to recharge our glasses then remember there's nothing to recharge them with.

You want to know the best it gets? Really, the best it gets?

Come on, I tell him, get your stupid jacket.

I'm further under than he is but I know the last thing he wants is a steering wheel to hold. I climb in the driver's side of Ti's Golf, fix the mirrors while Fynn hides his eyes behind a pair of aviators.

You don't want those. Anyway, you still look like you, just more of an arsehole. Everyone looks like an arsehole in aviators.

Right, he says, flinging them into the lantana.

Since Fynn left some Perth kids came down and reopened the Kingfisher Hotel. The smoke-damaged collection of taxidermied birds that made it through the 2009 fire (suspected arson) are still roosting about the liquor shelves. The fibre optic thing is still there, the pool table is still there. But the bar's been refitted, a big slab of reclaimed redgum – behind it the top tier stuff is seven tiers up, and the bartender has to put down his copy of the DSM-5 or whatever and hop a ladder to get to it.

These boys don't know Fynn. These boys will pour him his drink without asking just how he likes being back home.

We take bar seats opposite a singed black cockatoo, its glassy eye on the rum selection. Fynn wins the wallet race, the leather split like overripe pawpaw, gaping fifties.

You need to carry all that around?

From the Travelex. I closed all my accounts when I left Australia.

You really weren't planning on coming back, huh.

Guess I wasn't.

There are Fynn's hands, threaded mangrove-like around his glass. Roughened by work that has nothing to do with him, work that carries nothing of himself. In my shed there's a second table and a set of chairs and a bookshelf. In February it heats up to a million degrees in there – *six bloody summers* – all the wood has buckled and split along the joins, the wires gone slack or snapped, all that careful tension ruined. I should have kept them inside. I should have driven into Perth this morning, been there waiting when he hefted his bag off the carousel. Now it's all I can do to lift my pint glass and meet his.

Of course the guy was always going to appear, his company cap pulled low, eyes shaded from the glare of pool table fluorescents. It takes him a moment – I see it, my brother sees it – to register that it's really Fynn sitting here, and when he does it's as if all the doors have blown open at once, the air pressure changes that fast. And if the glasses in their corral don't shatter, and the stuffed birds don't take flight . . . if the tables don't upend of their own accord, it's only because of the steadying hand someone puts on the fella's shoulder, guiding him back to the game, to his shot, to the rip of felt as he jabs too hard with the cue, the crack of the white against the five and the grinding roll in the belly of the table as the ball is captured there.

'Shot, someone says. .

Fynn is already fumbling at the zip on his jacket.

Sit down, I tell him. Finish your drink.

Raf, we can't stay here.

Well, I'm finishing mine. I take a long, purposeful swallow to show him.

Fynn doesn't reach for his. Is he looking?

Christ, I'm not looking to see if he's looking.

I can't just sit here and pretend like ... I should go say something.

What's to say? I told you, there's nothing. Just finish your drink, for fuck's sake. (When what I'd meant to say was: Brother. Be still. We're okay here.)

Fynn sits down, visibly shrinking inside the jacket's bulk. I watch this, and I don't know what good I'm trying to force. Or even if it's good.

Right, I tell him, setting my glass beside his. You're right. Jiggety-jig.

The way home is all roadkill and scarpering night creatures – future roadkill – streaking through the high beams. Bundles of fluff and mashed feathers at the side of the road.

Acquitted, I remind him. Everyone knew it was not his intention to run three quarters of a family off a sandstone bluff. Everyone understood that. At least officially.

Okay, yes it's awful, it's tragic, but it wasn't your fault.

How much quiet is there before Fynn clears his throat and goes, Listen. Raf? There never was any dog.

I say, How do you mean, no dog? Because I had seen the dog. Just as clearly as if I'd been riding shotgun for that nightmare. Fynn's described it a hundred times – that mongrelly, grey-houndish thing, ribs on display through its sorry sack of grey skin. The way it skittered out of the scrub like a wraith. Looking back over its scrawny shoulder, as though something back there had spooked it senseless.

There just wasn't. I don't ... Can we leave it at that?

No, I think. No, we cannot leave it at that. But I drive the dark highway and keep quiet. Where had it gone then, the dog? Fynn had looked for it, in the first hundred versions of the story. He'd stood at the mangled safety barrier and called 000 – that part is fact; that part is on the record – and wondered, moronically, he said, where the fucking dog had got to. Because I wanted to kick it. His right knee bloody and ragged from where it had been crushed up against the ignition. A BAC of .03. Two beers, sober enough. This is also on the record.

If not the dog?

I roll us in silent to the driveway, past Fynn's rental car which has been tipped up on its side, exposing its shiny undercarriage. We get out and stand beside it without speaking for a moment, the air full of insect and sprinkler music.

Happens all the time, I lie. It's what these kids out here tip instead of cows.

How many people would that take?

Probably doesn't weigh much more than a cow. Should we flip it back?

It only takes a half-hearted shove. The car lands with a crunch that brings a flurry of curtain movement all up and down the street but nothing breaks and no one yells out. The passenger door is scraped up and the wing mirror is cactus.

Insurance?

Fynn just breathes in long and deep through his nose.

No way it's connected, this and the blokes at the bar. They were still there when we left. Just one of those freak coincidences. I'm saying all this to Fynn and he's saying nothing.

Inside, Ti has left the couch made up with sheets and pillows, and the coffee table – Fynn's coffee table – made up with a glass of water and a pack of aspirin.

Keeper, Fynn says, with a smile so pissweak I have to tell him g'night.

Ti gives a little moan as I slide in with her, fit my knees into the backs of hers. My chest against her spine, face pushed into her hair. Her hair smells like the ocean. I slide my hand between her thighs, not really to start something, just to be there, and we stay tangled like that, drifting nearer and further from sleep, until headlights flood the room.

It's nearly three a.m. when he shows up, swaying out there on the lawn. The father, the widower. So drunk he's practically dancing, a boxer or bear.

He pounds the door fit to unhinge it, but his voice is surprisingly soft when he says, It's not right. It's not right that it's me coming to you.

No, I hear Fynn answer. I know it's not.

There's the click of the screen door as he steps onto the verandah, before I can tell him, don't. Don't say shit. About the dog. About the complete lack of dog. He doesn't need to know.

I drag the sheet with me into the hallway, holding it around my waist. Through the flywire I watch the two of them cross the lawn towards the street, then further on into the night air, away from the house. Away from help. My brother wading out into the dark and the dark folding over the top of him like a wave. No right thing now, no best thing. Nothing so easy as lifting a child onto his shoulders and carrying her safely above the grabbing sea.

Nose Bleed

David Oberg

By the time I got to my mum's house I was already starting to think there might be something wrong with me and then Mum asked me how I was and I told her I have this cyst on my back that hurts when I touch it, and Mum said that's disgusting, that's disgusting, how are you going to find a husband if you keep talking like that, if you talk about your body like that, and I said Mum, I don't need to find a husband, I don't expect to find a husband anyway, I tend to only have sex with drunk guys, and Mum grimaced and told me that if I don't respect myself I'll never find a good man, and that if I just met a good man I wouldn't have to humiliate myself, and I said no, Mum, you don't understand, I only have sex with drunk guys because when I cum I make this guttural noise with my throat, it feels like it's coming from my stomach, like a kitchen sink when you drain the water, or like a dying toad, I've had it ever since I was a teenager and it's done nothing but escalate in volume and depth, when I lost my virginity the guys I was with were kind of grossed out, but drunk guys don't seem to notice it because they're drunk and they're usually already asleep by the time I cum, so we all get along, and Mum stood up and pointed to the door and said I told you not to talk like that, get out, and I said all right, and as I walked down the steps I called out and asked if she would prefer it if I lied to her and she said no, I don't want you to lie to me, I just wish you were different.

Anyway, I think whatever is wrong with me started when I was a little girl, back when my father died and I didn't cry at his funeral, before I developed the cyst on my back.

I didn't mind leaving my mum's house early because I was meeting Scott for coffee since it was my day off and the sooner the better because I wanted to see a movie afterwards, and I didn't mind Scott but he tended to talk a lot, he talked a lot after we had sex even though he was drunk, which was a shame, and although I considered us at the very least acquaintances, I think it's impossible to like everything about a person, especially if they run out of things to say, which at the rate Scott spoke was more than likely, and we met in the mall and he asked me how I was going so I told him about the cyst on my back and how my mum reacted when I told her about the noise I make when I cum and Scott said that's disgusting, you should see a doctor, and I wasn't sure if he wanted me to see a doctor because of the cyst or because of the noise I make when I cum but all I said was I don't need to see a doctor, and he said please, do it for me, and I laughed, and I don't think he liked that I laughed, and then Scott got really serious and he looked down at his chocolate milkshake with a degree of angst and he said do you ever feel bad about enjoying something?

Did I ever feel bad about enjoying something.

I knew what he was talking about. Feeling nothing when something good happens, never really being in the moment, someone tells you they love you and you aren't in the room. Sure, I understand that. I understand feeling like your default state is the point of origin on a graph, that no matter how far you go in any direction you'll always end up back at the beginning, feeling nothing. There's a happiness I haven't felt since I was a little girl and I think it is because I grew up, more than anything, and there's nothing wrong with that, but when I do something that used to make me happy but no longer does, I understand how that's upsetting. It works both ways. At my father's funeral I was elsewhere, and that made me feel like maybe there was something wrong with me.

Then Scott said I feel bad when I spend time with you, I enjoy spending time with you too much, and I said why the fuck do you feel bad about that? You should feel good about enjoying something, why the fuck would you feel bad? And he said no, no, you don't understand, I have feelings for you, I feel affection towards you, and I said I like it when people are affectionate towards me, it makes me feel good, and Scott said then do you want to be together, and I said no, not really, and he said I can make you happy, and I said what if I'm already happy, what if I don't want to be happy, and if you don't like being affectionate towards me then I think you should just stop having those feelings. He was definitely upset then, and he said something about how his emotions were valuable and I said, are you crying? and then he just got up and left, and I thought damn, I thought he would talk more, and now I have an hour to kill before the movie starts.

There was only one other person in the movie theatre, a fat woman who sat up the back eating popcorn. The trailers started to play and occasionally I would hear her high-pitched laughter from behind me whenever something silly happened onscreen. I started laughing too. Then we started yelling things out. That looks like shit. I love musicals. By the time the movie started we both got out of our seats and met in the middle. We watched the movie and riffed on it. We made fun of the story, pointed out plot holes, told the characters what to do and chastised them for disobeying. Then I got a nosebleed, and I put my hand to my face and said sorry, this hasn't happened since I was a little girl, and the woman told me not to worry, it was fine, and she handed me her handkerchief. She started to tell me about how her kid gets nosebleeds sometimes while I wiped my nose but then I started to gag, I had tipped my head too far back, and I coughed up a clot of blood covered in mucus into the handkerchief. I laughed loudly then because that'd never happened before. When I looked up at the fat woman she laughed too. She laughed with me, with my face covered in blood, and I didn't know if she was laughing out of shock or genuine amusement but I didn't feel the need to ask, nor did I feel the need to tell her about the cyst on my back or the noise I make when I cum, and I offered her the handkerchief back and she said no, no, you keep it. When the movie ended she left because she had to pick up her kid, the one with the nosebleeds, from school. I wondered if I would ever see her again.

I didn't know what to do with my afternoon so I went to the beach, I didn't really intend to swim or sunbathe or any of that shit, I just wanted to go there and be alone. When I got to the beach a storm was rolling in, and I could see families and couples fleeing up the sand dunes away from me. Then rain began to fall and the sky became completely grey and I could only see a few dozen metres in front of me because of the mist from the water and I thought finally, good, I am alone.

I walked out on the pier and held my arms around my chest as the wind beat my shirt and I was thinking about what Scott said about wanting to be together and I wondered what that even meant. Being together. The last time I remember being together with someone, outside of fucking drunk guys with drunk dicks, was at my father's funeral when my little sister held my hand so hard she cut into my skin with her nails. I didn't know she was strong enough to do that, but that day she was. She held on so hard I thought she'd never let go. Then the rain reached me. There was a build-up behind my eyes and I wanted to cry but I couldn't, I couldn't cry. I wanted to cry and I wished that I wanted to cry because my mother didn't understand me, and I wished that I wanted to cry because Scott thought he knew me, but the truth is I wanted to cry because I would never see the fat woman in the movie theatre ever again, and spending time with her was time without the expectation to fuck someone or to know someone and meeting her like that was the best it would ever be, it was the best it would ever be, because if I got to know her I would find something I didn't like, or I would find something I couldn't relate to, and maybe all we had in common was the handkerchief, and maybe that was enough for that moment, in that empty movie theatre, and at least I wasn't elsewhere for that, and I was sure she would find the same of me, and I wanted to cry so much as rain soaked me through, so I decided to just pretend to cry and hoped the tears would appear on their own. I scrunched up my face and turned my mouth down and started breathing really hard and making little wailing noises like people do when they cry and I watched the rain spill off my face and into the ocean mist and thought that if anyone could see me right now they wouldn't know I was pretending, they wouldn't know the difference, and I thought fuck, I need to go home, I'm saturated and I can't even cum, or cry, what's the fucking difference, so I walked back towards the city but I slipped on the pier and I

landed on my back and there was a sharp pain and a warm wetness that didn't match the rain falling around me and I made a
guttural gurgling noise with my throat and stomach that sounded
like dirty water going down a drain or a dying toad.

I was at work the next day when Scott walked in, which bothered
me because I doubted he actually wanted to buy any soap. He had
a real sour look on his face and I figured he was going through
that sulky stage that all good men go through when they're
rejected and trying to find a way to salvage their egos and he saw
me smiling and asked me what the hell was I so happy about, and
I said, you're looking at a girl who finally popped her cyst, and he
said, that's disgusting, and I said hey, you fucking asked.

The Telephone

John Kinsella

They were close enough to the dregs of the river to have a water rat dead on their dead lawn. The neighbouring boy, Vaughan, came over to poke a stick at it and say, My sister has *fur* like that, and snigger. When Joel set up a homemade phone 'network' between his room and Vaughan's sister's, it was to talk with Vaughan and not Nina. But he was short of copper wire, so until he could afford more and get down to the city to procure it, or come across a piece of old equipment he could strip down and acquire extra wire that way, it was Nina's room that served as the phone booth.

Theirs was one of the Five Towns that dotted the Avon River's winding way down through the valley. Their town was mostly dry and not much visited compared with a few of the others. The river seemed to run out of steam, or maybe just couldn't get restarted outside the town waterhole that had sort of survived the river's 'training', when the authorities dredged out the year-round waterholes the Noongar people had respected and benefited from. Maybe it was because the town was really closer to the river's beginning rather than its end.

Joel's interest in electronics at the age of twelve was not usual in the district, especially in 1974. Guns and sport were the main-stays of the local boys and surrounding farms. Hanging around the linesman renewing the powerlines through the town, Joel got a taste for electricity. The powerlines reached out over the paddocks and vanished before reappearing alongside the road to the next Avon Valley town. Though their town was small, it had a phone exchange, a transformer and streetlights. All of this excited and inspired him.

When he placed a ladder against the wall and window frame of Nina's room, Mr Scalpini roared at him. What are you doing there, son? Peeking at Nina?

No, sir, sorry, I'm just feeding these wires through the broken corner of the flywire. The window will still shut and everything.

And then Vaughan stuck his head out of the open window, through an even larger hole in the wrecked flywire panel, and said, It's okay, Dad, Nina said we could, and she's down at Vicky's place.

Mr Scalpini scratched his beard and said, Well, I guess it's okay. Just watch those damn asbestos panels, they crack just like that! He then vanished around the front of the house, and probably down to the pub. Joel was actually more astonished to see Mr Scalpini at home on a Saturday afternoon than at getting a blast from him.

Okay, Vaughan, pull the wires through and anchor them under a book or somethin' and I'll be in in a jiff to rig up the handset.

It'll be neato being able to talk in the middle of the night, Joel. I'll sneak in when Nina's snoring and we can whisper.

Yep, neato, neato.

The 'handset' consisted of two parts strung together – an ear-piece ripped out of an old phone, and a mouthpiece made from a built-in mike taken out of a cassette recorder. On the Scalpini side of the network, these pieces were it – bound together with tape and wire, liable to disconnect if care wasn't taken. Joel ran Vaughan through the steps, and through them again. The 'exchange' was on Joel's side, naturally – the *powerpack* (consisting of two nine-volt batteries), the on/off switch, and a secretive little package of solid-state electronics which Joel insisted were key to the network's success. He was designing a switchboard that would allow other neighbours to be added to the network if the prototype proved a success and some extra dosh came his way to buy bits and pieces. He had lots of stuff already – people were always giving him their broken electronic items. My *electronica*, he called it.

Vaughan was bursting to give it a go, but got stuck on why he didn't have a 'switch' on his side as well. You need to be trained, said Joel, and there can only be one *central* exchange.

Okay, Vaughan, you wait here, keep your ear to the phone, and I'll nip over to mine and give you a call.

Vaughan placed the earpiece so hard to his ear that he nearly pulled the flimsy wiring away. Come on, be careful. Gentle. You're like a bull in a china shop. Vaughan giggled at this, and stared out his sister's window, across the grey picket fence that divided the quarter-acre blocks, at Joel's window, which was a precise replica of his sister's but with the entire flywire panel removed. Both windows sat in a pale blue sea of painted asbestos.

Joel's head appeared in his window, with earpiece and mike at ear and mouth (his were a little more sturdy and looked as if much more love and care had gone into their making), and he waved his hand, which was followed by a crackling sound in Vaughan's earpiece and then a HELLO! so loud from Nina's room that it was heard four houses away.

I can hear you, Vaughan – no need to yell. This is sensitive 'quipment.

And so it began. They gibbered for hours. About nothing. They played their transistor radios 'over the line' for hours. Nina, wary and slightly disgusted, as if this kid boys' stuff was in some way contaminating, nonetheless talked stiffly with Joel's younger sister about *nothing*. Mrs Scalpini got on the line to talk to Joel's mother about the next P&C meeting. On Sunday just after lunch, Mr Scalpini asked Joel's dad if he wanted to go down to the session together; they were drinking mates who didn't fraternise at all outside the pub.

On the first night, Joel switched the system off because the batteries were running down and he wanted to save enough juice for talking on Sunday. But on Monday after school he went to the co-op and spent his remaining money on a bunch of new batteries.

School had been something – Vaughan, who was much more popular than Joel, had bragged to all the farm boys about how cool the phone was. Some of them said they'd like to give it a go, and Vaughan invited them, until Nina got wind of it and squashed it fast. As she was in second year at the District Junior High

School, she scared even the tough twelve-year-old boys shitless.
They gawked over her and made lewd jokes to her brother, which
he encouraged, but if she actually spoke to them, which was rare,
they quickly melted away. Grubby little sods, she said, they're not
going into my room!

They talked after dinner. Joel switched the exchange on and
heard Vaughan saying, Breaker, breaker ... You there? ...
Breaker, breaker ... How long have you been on there, Vaughan?
Ten minutes. Nina said she wants me out of the room asap, whatever that means.

Come off it, we've just got on. Hey, you're using CB language
when you say breaker, breaker.

Yeah, it's what Dad says during harvest when he's driving the
truck. Citizen Band Radio. Ten-eight. Or is it ten-nine? Whatever.

Gee, Vaughan, you're getting pretty smart in your old age.

Think so? Hey, did you see Jenny Harris fall on her bum today
and flash-a-gash?

You're disgusting, Vaughan!

Yeah, I am, ain't I? Whoo, I can hear Nina heading this way.
Vampire alert! She's yelling at Mum about the dishes and
homework.

That transducer ...

That what?

That mike is pretty good, pretty receptive ... I mean, I can
hear her carrying on. It picks up everything.

Neato! Anyway, I've got to scoot. Hangin' up now! Catch you
on air after school tomorrow. Be good when you get more wire
and it reaches my room. Then we can talk all night. It'll be
grouse, mate, grouse.

Joel went to say, Right, but heard the phone clunk to the
ground and get pushed aside – sounded like a shoe across the
carpet. Jeez, Vaughan, be careful! But Vaughan was gone with a
Scram! from Nina. And then there was walking and a click, and
crappy music started playing. Joel listened for a while, then worried about the batteries and switched the set off. He messed with
the set a bit, wondering about improvements, and wondering why
Vaughan used words like 'grouse' when he was going on about
nothing. But Mr Scalpini spoke like that. Little wonder, Joel's
mum would have said.

Late that night, Joel woke to yelling and carrying-on from next door. It wasn't unusual. Mr Scalpini had come in from the pub and was telling everyone what was what. Sometimes at school, away from the ears of their homes and street, Joel would quietly ask Vaughan what his old man's yelling in the middle of the night was about, but Vaughan would say, Ah, nothin', really ... just Dad lettin' off some steam. He always gave the same response.

And if Joel mentioned it to his mum or dad, they said in their curt voices, Mind ya business, Joel, and others will mind theirs. But it keeps me awake, he'd complain. And they'd say, Put the pillow over your head. Or, Invest in some cotton wool.

It went on and on. Normally, when he was woken and couldn't sleep, he thought up new inventions, or what he would hint at for birthday or Christmas. And then, when it all went deathly quiet, which it always did, he strained his ears to listen. To what, he wasn't sure. Sometimes he could hear a fox bark, and imagined it running through the shining crops that came right up to the back of their house. He could identify all the living sounds of the dark. One day, he'd record them.

Joel wasn't a stickybeak by nature. He kept pretty much to himself, other than mucking around with Vaughan, and that was only because they were neighbours and had a kind of deal whereby Joel helped Vaughan with difficult schoolwork and Vaughan kind of kept the farm boys off his case. Actually, Vaughan always let them go at Joel a bit, and giggled if they wedgied him. But eventually he would step in and say, 'Nuf's e-nuf, boys. Vaughan was huge. Mum says I'm overgrown for me age, he said fact-like to Joel.

Not a stickybeak, but for some strange reason, suddenly curious. Scientific-like. Investigative. He reached up for his torch, his 'faithful companion', slipped quietly out of bed and went to the phone set, switched it on, heard the low crackle of electric current and the workings of magnetism and coiled wire loud in the speaker, in the earpiece, then held his breath knowing the same sound would emerge across the fence in Nina's room. He placed the earpiece to his ear and a hankie over his mike to muffle the sound of his breathing and listened.

He could hear murmuring and rustling. He put the phone down gently, lifted out his seat, flicked the torch off, carefully pulled the corner of his curtain out, and looked across to Nina's window. There was a dull glow coming from around the curtain. It was a sickly orange colour. That'll be her bedside light. Maybe she's reading. He let his curtain fall back into place and with the torch, searched his desktop for his watch. It was one a.m.

Jeez, that's late to be reading, he thought. Maybe she's as good as Vaughan at reading and pronounces each word with her finger following underneath. Then he felt ashamed and shook his head.

He went back to the phone and almost switched it off, but heard a little cry and a clear *Don't!*, kind of sharp but quiet. He listened close. It's such a grouse patch of fur, it's so soft ... it's lovely. It wasn't Nina speaking. Joel felt sick and then just stopped himself yelling out, Leave her alone, Vaughan, you sicko! When he heard Mr Scalpini say loud and clear, Stop trying to block me, you silly little slut! Joel instantly switched off the phone, turned off the torch, and slunk towards his bed where he shivered, wide-awake, owl-eyed, through the rest of the night.

*

When Joel dismantled the phone because the batteries didn't last long enough and it wasn't a very good phone anyway, he didn't even ask for the wire and the handset to be returned from across the fence. Nah, Vaughan, you have them. Mementos. Vaughan looked disappointed and nonplussed, then grinned and said, Like souvenirs?

Yes, Vaughan.

Well, neato. Thanks – you're a real friend. A mate. I'll stop the boys giving you a wedgie, next time.

Joel was sitting alone in a shady, dull corner of the quadrangle eating his lunch as usual, yet not as usual, reading a comic book instead of an electronics book from the library, when Nina came up to him. She stood close, looked around to see who was watching, and said quietly, He heard that phone of yours crackle when you turned it on to eavesdrop on me.

Joel wanted to protest but his tongue wouldn't work properly.

He's got ears like a dog, even when he's drunk, she spat. I whispered to him, You better watch out because they'll know now, all of them will know what you're up to. I said to the old pig, Don't you know Joel tells his little sister everything and she tells her mum and dad everything. And then he tried again but I stopped him and he started to throttle me, Joel ... you didn't hear that, did you? You'd gone, hiding.

And with this she lifted a velvet band around her neck, which Joel had thought she wore because it made her look sexy, and he saw a livid purple ring going right round. I call it my halo, she said, laughing, smarter than her brother by a mile. Anyway, he's stopped, he's stopped everything. He got off me and went out and hasn't been near me since. He just grunts when spoken to. Oink oink! I know he won't be back.

Nina kicked at a bit of stone that had eased from the asphalt quadrangle during the summer and settled into no-man's-land over winter. She said, I know you think I'm a slut, but I'm not. Joel started to splutter fragments of sandwich over his book, his lunch box slipped out of his lap, and he stammered, No, never, no, I don't, I am really sorry.

And then Nina leant down, kissed Joel on the top of the head, turned, walked off, and did not speak to him again.

Growth

Mirandi Riwoe

It lies on the crisp hospital sheet, absolutely grotesque. Dr Arnold tells us it's called a *fetus in fetu*. Our son's unformed twin. Most likely joined via the umbilical cord in gestation, now just a jumble of elephantine bone and skin, about the size of an apricot. Three canines – there's no denying they're teeth – protrude in a jagged line across its circumference. When we first saw it after the operation there was a shock of hair pressed to its side, still moist from having Thomas's stomach juices washed away. It looked like the slick of hair and scum drawn from a shower's plughole. I gagged, felt nausea water my mouth. But the hair, the colour of wheat and nearly ten centimetres long, is dry now, almost glossy. It looks like her hair. Like Hannah's.

'It's been living in Tom's abdomen,' says the doctor, glancing over to where Thomas lies asleep, in recovery. 'He should be good to go in a couple of days. No more tummy upsets. No more vomiting.'

'What do you mean "living"?' asks Paul.

Dr Arnold purses her pale lips, considers what to say. 'It's been growing inside Tom's stomach, growing with him.'

'Like a parasite?' The distaste on his face the same as when he changes nappies.

Dr Arnold bobs her head side to side, a little like the bobble-head dog we used to have on the dash of the Holden. 'Yes. I guess so. A parasite.'

'What will you do with it?' I ask her.

The doctor bends down, scrutinises the small mass. 'They're extremely rare, you know.' She's far more interested in it now than in our son. Her blond hair is in a high ponytail, has a navy blue ribbon tied in a bow. I wonder if she has a neat row of ribbons arranged on her dresser, a rainbow to choose from according to her outfit. She says, 'I don't think it'll be destroyed. I'm sure the research team would like to have a gander at it.'

'But I'd like to keep it.' I haven't given the words any thought. I watch surprise lift the doctor's brow, the recoil of my husband. 'It was part of Thomas. You said it yourself.'

'Yeah, as a parasite, Shelly. Get it together.' Paul smirks towards the doctor.

At least it survived, I think.

*

I'm wrapping salad sandwiches in the school tuckshop when I get the call to say I can finally pick up the twin. That's what I've started to call it in my head. But not to Paul. He's already joked that he wouldn't be surprised if I gave the parasite a name. He was only half-joking, though. There was contempt in his voice, too, like when he points out the flab that mushrooms over the waist of my jeans, or when he catches me watching *Home and Away*.

I want to peel off my disposable gloves, shove the squares of sandwich paper over to the next mum, but it's nearly eleven o'clock, time to deliver the baskets of food. The other mums already think I'm a bit of a cow, a bit stand-offish, but it's just that I don't have the time or money to hang out with them. I listen to their talk of trips to Fiji or Sydney, and the packages they receive from stores in the USA, but what do I have to add? The only reason I'm here is to see Thomas's smile when he hands me a sticky coin for a fluorescent ice-block.

I have to pick the twin up from the hospital's pathology centre. The woman on reception pulls the jar from a zip-lock bag, and the twin is awash in formalin.

'What a gruesome little creature, huh?' She laughs. 'I bet your son was glad to be rid of it.'

I'm sorry that it's not dry anymore, that the length of wheat hair is no longer glossy. The hair is darker in the jar, like seaweed, floating around its host.

When I arrive home I'm not quite sure what to do with it. I place the jar on the deck table, and the formalin takes on the bottle-green of the table's surface. Thomas is delighted with it when Paul brings him home from school. He shakes the jar, so that the teeth clank against the plastic. I want to stop him, but Paul's with him, and they are both studying it like it's a science experiment. I watch them through the kitchen window as I prepare a salad for dinner. I follow the recipe I found in a magazine. I have the rocket and haloumi, but not the pomegranate. My salad looks a little bereft without the gleaming ruby seeds, but who on earth can afford a pomegranate at four dollars a pop?

'Can I take it to school?' asks Thomas.

'Of course, mate,' says Paul. 'How cool will it be to tell everyone this is the twin you gobbled up in Mummy's tummy?'

Paul grabs Thomas's stomach, wobbles it, until Thomas squeals. But then Paul sees my face.

He comes to my side, rests his hand on my shoulder. It's reassuring, but has weight too. 'It's not real, you know. It was never a real ... You know.'

I shrug off his hand, slice the haloumi. 'I think we should bury it.'

'Bury it?'

'Yeah.' I think of the flat grounds of the crematorium. The straggly rose bushes, the square plaques. 'Yeah. In the backyard maybe.'

'Like the guinea pig?' He's grinning at me now.

'Yeah. Maybe.'

Paul calls Thomas in for a bath, and while the chops are in the griller, I return to the deck, pick up the jar.

I stare at it for a long while and, not for the first time, wonder if it was a boy or a girl. Its hair is not as dark as Thomas's, so for that reason alone I think maybe it was a girl. Another daughter I've been robbed of.

*

For a few months after Hannah was born I didn't want her. Before that, when I was pregnant, I thought I was ready for children. Thought life with a baby was going to be like in those nappy advertisements, full of a carefree love as soft and sweet as talcum powder. But then the pulsing wound that surged against stitches, the sore bosoms as taut as balloons. Splinters of resentment lodged under my skin for that poor baby, whose cheeks held the blush of a seashell, whose earlobes were as velvety as a peach. I wasn't prepared for how truly potty I became from lack of sleep. It took a while for my skittling thoughts to gather, to grasp the fact that I wasn't Shelly anymore. I'd shifted. I had become Hannah's mum.

*

I can't sleep well again. I listen to the clock tick, to Paul's snoring. I lie still, let sweat prickle my scalp. But at least I'm not in pain anymore, not physical pain like after the car accident. I should ask my doctor for more sleeping pills, but I've always felt like that's cheating, like I'm trying to shut out memories of her.

I also spend hours wondering what the twin would have looked like had she survived. Would she have had Hannah's thin face, or Thomas's more sturdy features? Hannah's hazel eyes or Thomas's blue ones? And I fret about what to do if we ever move house. Will we dig up the twin from where we buried her in the yard?

After Thomas had his day of show and tell, Paul took me to Bunnings to choose a plant to bury the twin under. He wouldn't let me get a citrus, said it was gross, said he wouldn't eat the fruit from the parasite's tree. And anyway, it was too expensive. So I chose something called a plectranthus that had little bell-shaped flowers in angel pink. I thought that was appropriate. It was on special for eight dollars.

The soil in our yard is dry and stubborn. I chose a spot behind the mulberry tree, and my little garden spade chiselled against rocks and roots, but I couldn't ask Paul for help. Finally, I had a hole deep enough. I inspected the twin one last time, a swirl of flesh and hair, and then nestled the jar deep into the ground. I pushed the dirt back into the hole, leaving enough room to plant the plectranthus. And then I leaned over it, my palms resting against the ground. I didn't cry.

*

We take Thomas back to Dr Arnold for a check-up. She's wearing a purple ribbon this time, to match the pinstripe in her blouse. She's pleased with Thomas's progress, pleased he's finally put on a little weight.

'Did you ever pick up the specimen we found in his stomach?' she asks us.

I nod.

'Did they tell you it was just a teratoma, after all? Not a fetus in fetu.'

I can only stare. It's Paul who asks her what she means.

'It can be difficult to tell them apart, you see,' she says. 'A teratoma is a tumour. It's made up of various tissues, which is why it can resemble a fetus in fetu. But when pathology had a look at the mass we found in Thomas's stomach, they couldn't detect a spine or other organ matter. So they think it was only a teratoma.'

My mouth is open, but no words come. The doctor pushes her hand across the surface of her desk towards me. 'Don't worry, Shelly. It was benign. Nothing to worry about.'

'But the teeth? The hair?'

Her head bobs from side to side. 'Yes. Common.'

I smile. I don't know how to respond. There's an uncertain frown on Paul's face. Thomas flicks through a Thomas the Tank Engine book.

On the drive home I look out the window, squish as close to the passenger door as possible. The tips of my ears feel hot, as I wait for Paul to tease me. I buried a tumour in the backyard.

As soon as we pull into the driveway I stride through to the back, and unfurl the hose from its rack. I turn it on full blast and yank it over to the plectranthus. Its plump leaves wilt under the midday sun and the flowers have taken on a pulpy, brown tinge. I need to soften the soil, dig it up. The water pools on top of the tough dirt, refuses to sink in.

'Shelly, what're you doing?'

I stare at Paul. I can see he's on the edge. He teeters between sarcasm and concern. But I feel as hard as the soil, as barren. 'I'm digging up the teratoma.'

'You don't have to do that, honey. Just leave it.'

I shake my head. 'No. I don't need the reminder.'

'The reminder of what?'

The sun's rays sting the back of my neck. 'Of what I've lost.'

'But, baby, you never had it in the first place.'

I fall onto my knees and tear at the soil, rip my fingernails into it. The soil is damp at first, but dry dirt beneath. I rest back on my haunches. My shoulders are shaking. I'm laughing.

Numb

Myfanwy McDonald

I ride down to the shops on my father's bicycle. A white Peugeot racer with rusty gears. He can't balance on a bicycle anymore. He can barely balance on his own two feet.

At the counter, a woman wearing large, thick-lensed glasses flicks through a pile of envelopes packed tightly in a box. 'Yes?' she says, without looking up.

'I need a passport photo,' I say.

'Well, you'll have to wait.' She sighs, nodding at a chair in the corner. I look at myself in the mirror behind her. That face is not mine.

*

A few weeks later, my father arrives home from work, puts down his briefcase, loosens his tie and hands me the passport. The gold insignia on the cover features an emu and a kangaroo holding up a shield.

'Did you get it?' my mother says to him, stirring a pot on the stove.

'I just gave it to her,' my father replies as he's walking out the kitchen door.

Behind the cover of the passport is the photograph. 'It doesn't look like me,' I say, holding it up to show my mother. Her face is hidden behind a cloud of steam as she tips the contents of the saucepan into a colander. 'It doesn't look like me,' I say again quietly, to myself.

I dream sometimes that my tongue has been cut out of my mouth. Like an oyster shucked from its shell.

*

On the plane I stick the two-pronged headphone jack into the holes at the end of the armrest. Flick between the channels. Classical. Opera. Man talking. Middle of the road. Woman talking. Love songs. Country.

My father is sifting through a wad of old letters. He passes one to me and says something, pointing to the top of the page.

'What?' I say, pulling off the headphones.

'People usually don't say "what".' My father takes the letter back and peers at it again, frowning. 'They say "pardon".'

'What is it?' I lean over the armrest and he points again to the top of the letter, where part of the page has been ripped off. 'They tore off the address. Someone didn't want us to find her.'

'Find who?'

'My cousin. Adopted out.' The air hostess hands my father a warm bread roll with a pair of tongs, then starts serving the people in front of us. 'I guess you miss out,' my father says, shrugging, splitting the roll in two and handing me half.

*

'It was a submerged continent,' my father says after we've picked up the hire car. 'A long time ago. Then there were volcanoes and it just kind of came up, well, kind of … emerged, out of the ocean.' He holds his hand in a fist, then opens it like a flower.

His hands are thick and square, like giant blocks of cheese. Years ago, when he first got sick, I'd rub them: his thick, square hands. He said it helped. Made them feel less numb. Keeping his hands awake. Keeping his hands alive.

'Won't be long now,' my father says, reaching over and ruffling my hair.

We drive around the harbour. I watch white sails billowing in the wind.

*

It takes a few hours to get to where we're going. We turn onto a dirt road that cuts through a forest of mangroves. Gnarled black branches grow out of the shallow emerald water like deformed limbs. We emerge at a wide, calm body of water. Overlooking the water is a scattering of single-storey houses. Boxes dropped randomly onto the slope of a smooth green hill.

As we drive past the houses, people wave at my father from their porches. Raise their walking sticks in recognition. A white horse ambles by. A girl on top of it. My father waves at the girl. She doesn't wave back. 'You're probably related to her,' my father says. 'You're related to almost everyone on this road.'

I have never been here before. And I don't know any of these people.

*

'This your boy?' the old woman says as she shuffles around her kitchen in a pair of worn pink slippers.

'Girl. She's a girl. My youngest.'

We're sitting at a wooden table covered with a lace tablecloth. From the window, I can see the water, extending out towards distant green hills.

'Do you want something? Tea? Cordial? Milo?'

'Milo is fine,' my father says.

'Cat got her tongue?' the old woman says, placing a saucepan on the stove.

'This is my aunt,' my father says to me, pointing at her. He's speaking slowly, carefully, leaning close – as if I'm much younger than I actually am. 'Aunty Jean. Your great-aunt. My mother's sister. We'll be staying with her for a few days.'

The Milo is mixed with water, rather than milk. It tastes strange. 'Drink it,' my father hisses at me under his breath and points at the mug. 'Just drink it.'

Underneath the lace tablecloth I see deep grooves etched into the edge of the table. As if someone has taken to it with an axe.

*

'You'd look exactly like your father. If you were a boy,' my mother said last summer. I was sitting in the back seat of the car, worrying about the tampon. It was the first time I'd used one. It had been in for too long, and I thought I might die of toxic shock syndrome.

The first time I saw a tampon I was shocked by how big it was. I was expecting something inconspicuous, capsule-like. But it was as big as a bullet.

*

I'm lying in my great-aunt's bed. 'What took you so long?' she wails in the room next door. 'How long has it been? Ten years?'

'I've got a family,' I hear my father say. 'You know it's hard to get away, Jean.'

'Your family is here,' my great-aunt replies. 'Your whole family is here.'

'It's not his fault he's married to an Australian,' someone calls out. Laughter. Then a guitar, and singing. I hear my father's voice: high-pitched, faltering, melancholy.

Later my father slips into bed beside me. It is the only bed in the house. My great-aunt is going to sleep on the couch with her grandchildren.

'No, no,' my father said to Aunty Jean when she suggested it. 'We're not going to take your bed.'

'I'm your aunty. And you'll do what I say.' She poked him in the arm and he held his hands up in surrender.

My father lies so close to the edge of the bed, I worry he might fall. He's so quiet, I wonder if he sleeps at all.

*

The next day one of my father's cousins takes us fishing in his dinghy. The cousins have chests like barrels. Thighs like tree trunks. This one looks a bit like my father. The same high, thin forehead. The same small, shell-like ears. But my father is slighter. Paler. And he doesn't smile quite so easily.

The water sloshes up against the side of the boat. My father's cousin throws in his line. 'Throw it,' he says to me, nodding towards the water.

The boat rocks gently. My father is struggling to put the bait on the hook. Numb hands. But he's turned away, so his cousin cannot see that this task, this simple task, is too difficult for him.

A bite. I pull up the line and see a fish hanging from the end of it. 'Warehou,' my father says, looking over the edge of the boat. His cousin takes the hook out of its mouth and throws the fish onto a blue tarpaulin he's laid on the bottom of the dinghy. The fish flips over a few times. Tensing and relaxing its body like a fist. I throw the line back in. Catch another fish. And another. 'This must be in your blood.' My father smiles. And I'm thinking about fish. Swimming in blood. Trapped beneath the skin.

'Am I white?' I say to him later, as we walk up to the house.

'You're you,' he replies.

I walk behind my father as he climbs the stairs. I imagine that if he falls, I might be able to catch him. He clutches the wobbly wooden banister. His left foot hits the edge of each step with a dull thump. He grabs the handle of the screen door, pushes it open with his fist. A crowd of people are gathered in my great-aunt's house. The television on. Someone strumming the guitar. Brown bottles lined up on the coffee table.

'Here he is,' my great-aunt shouts. 'My favourite nephew.'

I turn around and walk back down the stairs. I don't know any of these people.

Down at the water I squat behind a bush. See the stain on the inside of my pants. Blood starts gushing out of me like a blubbering tap. I have nothing to soak it up. And I am too ashamed to ask. I walk back to the house. Climb through the window. Lie on the bed. I'm thinking of blood. A strip of blood down the back of a white horse. There's something about blood I don't understand. Something about my body I don't really want.

*

My father was looking for someone. And he found her. The cousin who was adopted out. 'How many cousins have you actually got?' I ask.

'Fifty?' he replies. 'Officially. Fifty-one, I guess, if you include this one.'

This cousin wrote to my father's father years ago to find out more about the family who had renounced her. My grandfather never replied. He was the one who ripped the return address off the top of the letter, so no one else from the family could contact her either.

On the way to visiting the long-lost cousin, we stop at a statue on a roundabout in a quiet country town. 'Your great-great-great-great-grandfather,' my father says, pointing to the stone man standing on his plinth. He's holding a weapon in one hand – shaped like a small flat violin – and in the other he's clutching the edge of his feathered cloak.

'You know how they used this weapon?' my father says.

I shake my head. I'm thinking about a girl I know at school, and the way she sometimes hugs me if she hasn't seen me for a while. I'm thinking about how I shrug her off, pretending I am averse to affection, all the while longing for her to do it again.

'Slice the top of the head off,' my father says, making a sharp, swiping motion with his hand. 'Like cutting the top off a boiled egg.'

I avoid the girl at school sometimes, for days. Just so when I see her again, she'll put her arm around me.

*

The long-lost cousin looks nothing like my father. She has frizzy hair and freckles. Orange eyes that match the colour of her hair. Her plump hands are the colour of pork sausages. They shake as she pours tea into a flowery teacup, passes around a small jug of curdled milk. Her house smells like wet dog.

'I don't think my father – your uncle – knew what to say,' my father says to her. 'When you wrote to him.'

The woman nods. Sits down on the edge of the chair. 'I understand.'

My father reaches for his cousin's pale hand and clutches it tightly. 'I'm sorry he never replied.'

'Not your fault,' the woman whispers. The three of us finish our tea in silence.

'Is she white?' I say to my father when we get back into the car.

'She's a cousin on my father's side. The Scottish ones.' He

sighs and rubs his face. 'They came over in droves, a century or
so ago, to tend their sheep.'

'She's quiet,' I say.

'Mm,' he says, turning the key in the ignition. 'Must be lonely.
Living alone in that dusty old house.'

*

'Don't touch it,' my father says, pointing to the electric fence.
'You'll hurt yourself.' Behind the fence is a field of horses. The
white horse approaches and looks at me. Its eyes are like black
holes in space. It bares its teeth in a grimace and throws its head
up and down a few times; its flapping gums sound like a wet tennis ball hitting a wall.

My father walks further up the hill, one hand underneath his
thigh to keep his leg from dragging. He stands at the top, pointing to the mountains on the other side of the harbour. He's
shouting something, but it gets lost in the swirling wind.

I touch the electric fence with my hand. The zap is a mean flat
buzz. Almost clinical.

'Why did you do that?' my father says later, shaking his head,
holding my hand in his. 'I told you not to touch it.' We're standing beneath this tree. And my father is squeezing my fingers,
then my hand. The way I used to for him. When he first got
sick. When he stopped riding his white Peugeot racer. The doctors couldn't tell him what was wrong with his giant, numb
hands.

I look at my hands sometimes and worry. 'You have a slightly
higher risk than the average person', the doctor said when I
asked him what I might inherit. 'But let's do a quick check.' I got
up on the examining bed and he told me to close my eyes. 'Tell
me when you feel it', he said, touching the tips of my fingers with
something soft, something sharp, something cold.

I was thinking of the girl. Imagining that it was her standing
between my legs, paying my body such intricate attention.

'Now, now. I can feel it now,' I kept saying.

*

On the way back to the city, we stop to visit the long-lost cousin again. When we get there, my father reaches over and takes an envelope from the glove box. Opens it and pulls a sheet of paper out, lays it on the dashboard.

'Family tree,' he says, surveying the piece of paper, as if it were a map. 'There's you, see?' Me. A circle. The daughter of a square. 'And here's my father.' He traces the line and taps on his father's name twice. 'And his brother,' running his finger along the horizontal line. 'And this is where she should be,' he says, tapping the empty space beneath his uncle.

'Thought she might like a copy,' he says, checking his reflection in the rear-vision mirror, wiping his thin hair to one side of his forehead. 'You can stay here,' he says. 'Won't be long.'

I fiddle with the car stereo. Flick through the radio stations. Then I pull out the postcards I bought. I promised the girl from school I would write to her, but I can't think of what to say, so I draw a picture of her and me but it looks stupid, so I tear up the postcard and start to write another. But I make a mistake and when I try to cross it out, it leaves a smudge and it looks like I've tried too hard. So I tear that postcard up too. I peer out the window and look for my father. The front door is open. A dog trots out of the house and sniffs at the lawn.

A man and a woman walk past the house. They're joking with each other – he's trying to grab her and she's pushing him away, laughing. I'm thinking of the time the girl from school got drunk at a party by the beach. She hung off my shoulder in the same way. It started to rain so we hid beneath an upturned dinghy. She ran her fingers along the inside of my arm, and at that moment I was glad to have a body. A body that could feel.

In the rear-vision mirror I see an ambulance. It's driving down the street quietly. No sirens. It pulls in behind our car. My father emerges from the house, waves at the ambulance driver then disappears back inside.

I open the car door and walk down the path. The paramedics enter the house. My father is standing in the hallway, leaning against the wall.

'Vera?' I hear the paramedics calling, their boots thumping heavily on the wooden floorboards. 'Vera?'

'What happened?' I say.

'Stay there!' my father shouts. 'Don't come in.'

The paramedics are now crouched over at the end of the hall-way, facing the dining room. I can't see her from where I'm standing.

'Stay there,' my father says again.

'What have you taken, Vera?' the paramedics are saying. 'Stay with us, love. What have you taken?'

*

We've stopped at a service station cafe. My father is cutting up a piece of fluorescent yellow cake with a fork. 'People hurt them-selves sometimes,' my father says. 'She'll be okay. They've taken her to hospital.'

I'm thinking of the girl again. The way she pulls me in towards her, her arm wrapped around my neck. And the way I fight it, and the way she holds me even tighter. And how it feels when the game is over, and she's gone again.

My father reaches over and clutches my hands in his. 'Don't worry,' he says. My father's hands. These giant numb creatures I once brought back to life.

Polly Stepford (1932–1997)

Ryan O'Neill

Labor is not working. Labor is not working. Labor is not working.
From a speech at a Liberal Party Fundraiser in Sydney,
May 1985

Liberal Party politician Polly Stepford was born Pauline Lord in
the Western Sydney suburb of Baynton on 25 August 1932. She
came from an influential family; her mother Antonia was a well-
known socialite and her father Otto was president of the local
branch of the Liberal Party. As well as this, Otto owned over fifty
properties around the city, most of them in a state of such squalor
that the *Daily Trumpet* had named him 'Slum' Lord in the 1920s.
Polly was educated at a private girls' school, before commencing
an economics degree at the University of Sydney in 1949. It was
here that she joined the Australian Liberal Students Federation,
penning articles for the organisation's newsletter and quickly
making a name for herself as a formidable debater. Polly was less
successful in her academic studies, failing all of her first-year
subjects. Shortly before resitting her exams, which Polly passed
with flying colours, her father donated $50,000 to the universi-
ty's infrastructure development fund. Polly was never to fail
another subject.

Polly attended lectures rarely, spending time instead in her
role as treasurer for the Australian Liberal Students Federation,
and writing and rehearsing speeches for their debating team.

Her oratorical style was powerful, if robotic, and mostly consisted of repeating long strings of facts to confuse her opponents; if that did not work, she would compare them to Adolf Hitler, and this was almost always enough to clinch victory. She was only ever bested once, in a debate held in her third year at university in which she spoke in support of the proposition, 'A woman's place is in the home.' Her opponent was a brilliant young Marxist called Mick McCelty, a journalism student taking part in his first debate, and he comprehensively demolished Polly's arguments. That night, as McCelty celebrated his victory in the Students' Union, he was gravely injured after falling down a flight of stairs, and was left permanently paralysed. His accusation that Polly Lord had crept up behind him and pushed him was derided by her allies as class warfare. The resulting police investigation brought no charges against Polly; her alibi, that she was not on campus at the time of the accident, was supported by a dozen fellow Liberal students.

Polly graduated with a first class degree in 1952, leaving university just before the collapse of the Australian Liberal Students Federation, amid claims of gross financial mismanagement. After four years working for her father's firm, she stood successfully as a Liberal councillor for Baynton in 1956; at only twenty-four she was the youngest councillor in the country's history. From the first, her stridently pro-business agenda found many friends outside the council chamber, but few within, where Labor councillors accused her of bullying and intimidation. Polly was particularly active in spearheading reforms to the council's Planning and Development Approvals Process, slashing the processing time for applications from nine months to just three days. She was also instrumental in helping to push through several massive building developments which required the demolition of a number of historic buildings, despite strident local opposition. In May 1960, after her landslide re-election, Polly was made mayor of Baynton, and shortly afterwards she married Martin Stepford, a protégé of her father's who had made his fortune from the developments that Polly had ensured were approved. Despite repeated demands from opposition councillors for an enquiry into the Stepfords' business dealings, and controversy over the mayor's rapidly ballooning expenses, which included the hire of a limousine to travel fifty metres, Polly Stepford successfully quashed any questioning of her authority. The *Baynton Advertiser*, recently purchased by her father, was a staunch supporter of the mayor, especially after the sacking of its editor, Mick McCelty.

Stepford weathered an increasing number of political storms over the next few years, but her tenure as mayor came to an end in September 1969 with Baynton Council's bankruptcy. The council had been tied up in litigation for nearly two years over a parking ticket that had been given to local resident Mick McCelty, now a broadcaster for the ABC. McCelty had been given the ticket for parking in a disabled space, despite displaying the appropriate permit, and he alleged that the mayor had instructed the council parking inspectors to harass him, a claim that was eventually upheld in court. The substantial damages awarded to McCelty came amid reports of serious financial irregularities in the council's accounts, which eventually led to the appointment of administrators and the resignation of the mayor. Stepford claimed that she had been exonerated when an independent report on the debacle was released, despite it explicitly blaming her for the council's enormous financial losses. By then Stepford had become a director in her husband's company, Stepford PLC. The couple's already sizeable personal fortune increased rapidly after 1971 when Stepford PLC become Australia's only importer of 'Miracowall', a remarkably cheap, durable fireproof material used in plasterboard.

After her father's death in 1970, Polly Stepford took over his position as president of the local branch of the Liberal party, and in 1974 she was nominated to stand for the seat of Baynton in the federal election. Her campaign was notable for her absolute adherence to the party line, and even achieved a measure of notoriety when a linguist at Newcastle University released an analysis of all Stepford's speeches and interviews in a one-year period, and found that she never used a word that did not appear in the Liberal Party's election manifesto. Her oratory, which had become ever more mechanical since her student days, earned her the nickname of 'The Stepford Wife' from bored journalists.

After the Liberal victory in 1974, Stepford was made Deputy Minister for Education, and despite a blatant conflict of interest

exposed by Mick McCelty in ABC's *45 Minutes,* her husband's
company was awarded contracts to build dozens of primary
school buildings throughout the country, undercutting other
tenders by more than half thanks to the revolutionary Miracowall.
Stepford proved a capable deputy, and her unwavering loyalty
was rewarded in a 1980 cabinet reshuffle when she was promoted
to Education Minister. For a brief time she was embraced as an
icon for the feminist movement, but Stepford was quick to distance herself from feminism, insisting she had gotten to where
she was by hard work, and had never encountered sexism in her
life. Her heightened media profile saw her being interviewed
more often, which only served to reveal her disconnectedness
from her constituents; Stepford was in the habit of deploying
bizarre idioms such as 'Don't pass the potato' which she believed
ordinary Australians used.

Stepford's greatest strength lay in her adeptness at not answering questions. In one hour-long ABC interview, every question,
including 'How are you today, Minister?' and 'You were close to
your father; how did his death affect you?' was steered to the
topic of the Labor Party's plan to raise taxes. In opposition after
1983 Stepford was credited with pioneering the use of the 'four-
word slogan', a rhetorical device later embraced and finessed by
Tony Abbott. At a Liberal Party fundraiser in 1985, Stepford's
barnstorming thirty-minute speech consisted of only four words,
'Labor is not working', which she repeated, to increasingly frenzied applause, more than one hundred and eighty times. The
Liberal Party briefly adopted her slogan until it was revealed that
it had been plagiarised from the British Conservative Party's
1979 election campaign. This furore, however, was as nothing
compared to the scandal which erupted in 1986, and which
threatened to destroy Stepford's political career.

In July of that year, ABC's flagship current affairs show *Triangle*
broke the story of a huge unexplained spike in cases of childhood
leukaemia throughout Australia. Thanks to the tireless research
of Mick McCelty and his team, the cause of this increase was eventually traced back to Miracowall, which Stepford PLC had used
in the construction and renovation of primary schools in the
1970s; the material was found to be riddled with carcinogens.
Over the next five years, over three thousand children were

hospitalised and received radiotherapy, and more than a hundred died. The removal of Miracowall from the nation's schools cost hundreds of millions of dollars. Martin Stepford was arrested in November 1986 after releasing a statement that he alone was to blame for the Miracowall disaster. After just a week in custody, he died from a heart attack. Polly Stepford was only saved from arrest by a fire that destroyed most of Stepford PLC's records. She insisted she had done nothing wrong, but she could not ignore the national outrage and calls for her resignation. Finally, in January 1987, Stepford released a three-thousand-word statement of apology, which did not include the words 'sorry' or 'apologise'. She resigned from parliament two days later.

Stepford disappeared from public life for several years, gradually rebuilding her support in the party, and emerging once again to run for the seat of Baynton in 1993 after a federal enquiry into the Miracowall scandal, which Labor had boycotted, cleared her of any wrongdoing. Stepford began the campaign twenty points behind Labor in the polls, and she had been all but written off before deciding on a new strategy. Aware of a growing intolerance in Australian public life, Stepford became adept at exploiting it for her own ends, after a few false starts. At first, Stepford insisted there were too many Italians in Australia who were on benefits and stealing jobs, but when polling showed this line was not working, she moved on to the Greeks, with a similar lack of success. At last she settled on demonising Asians, which saw her popularity soar. Stepford's dog whistling proved popular not only in Baynton but around the country, as did her new catchphrase, beginning every sentence in interviews with 'As a battler myself ...' Not even her faux pas of attempting to eat a Chiko roll with a knife and fork at a photo op could dent her popularity.

Bankrolled by the coal and gas industries, Stepford outspent her opponent by a factor of three and was re-elected with a massive majority, despite the many protests reminding the public of her role in the Miracowall scandal. Stepford was appointed Deputy Minister at the Department of the Environment, and immediately set about rolling back environmental protection legislation. She became the darling of the party's hard right faction and in 1994, the *Daily Trumpet* predicted she would become

Australia's first female prime minister by the end of the decade. But this was not to be. In June of that year, Stepford claimed $250,000 on her parliamentary expenses for the renovation of her Baynton offices. After almost a year of investigations, Mick McCelty revealed on ABC News that only $10,000 of the money had gone to the builder; Stepford had kept the remainder for herself. Once again facing calls for her to resign, Stepford gave a tearful interview to *45 Minutes*, claiming that she had always been a feminist, and McCelty's lifelong persecution of her was simply because she was a woman.

Stepford's gambit failed, and a month later, with ill grace, she resigned and went to the back benches, announcing her retirement from politics at the next election. In a January 1997 interview with *Coal* magazine, Stepford spoke of the lucrative offers made to her to become a consultant for the coal industry, while simultaneously hinting at a return to politics. In February Stepford became ill, and was hospitalised due to breathing difficulties. Though she had never smoked, she was diagnosed with stage-four lung cancer and she died in hospital on 14 April 1997. A routine Health and Safety inspection of her Baynton office shortly after revealed her cause of death; Stepford had given so little money to the builder for the 1994 renovations of her offices that he had used the cheapest material he could find: Miracowall.

A United Front

Raelee Chapman

He finds his sister standing against the window. Sunlight is streaming in, her forehead pressed to the glass. Her loose hospital gown exposes her naked back, shoulderblades jutting like wings either side of her knotted spine. In the room are four beds stripped down to their rubber mattresses. A trolley of clean linen is parked near the door.

'Trace,' Luke calls, stepping around the trolley.

She walks over for a hug, keeping herself at arm's length so that they hug the air between them, barely touching each other. A male cleaner is shuffling about outside the room, waiting to get in, the pine-fresh smell of his mop bucket permeating the air. The ward is quiet, apart from the loud hum of the air conditioner blowing above Luke's head. He asks after the baby.

'He's in the nursery,' Tracey says, sitting down on an unmade bed, swinging her legs up onto it, exhausted. He waits for her to say more but she lies down, closes her eyes, and turns away from him.

*

Last Christmas, when Luke came home from uni, Tracey told them she was pregnant. They had just finished eating and debris from their meal cluttered the table: turkey bones, soiled napkins, torn bon bons and limp crepe-paper crowns.

'Jesus,' was all Luke said.

'Well, ain't that something. I'm going to be a young gran.' Their mother elbowed their father, taking three quick sips from a West Coast Cooler.

'You're still young, Trace. What about your job?' their dad said quietly. Tracey had been working at Kmart since she left school in Year 10; there was talk of a promotion – assistant manager.

'You were only eighteen when you had us,' Tracey said, rocking back on her chair.

She was nursing a premixed can of Jim Beam and Cola. Luke glanced at the can and raised his eyebrows at no one in particular. He wondered why his parents weren't asking who the father was but decided to keep his mouth shut. Maybe they knew something he didn't.

'We didn't plan to have kids so young, especially not twins. It was a shock. It meant making sacrifices,' their father said.

The light outside the dining room window was falling; soon his mother would draw the blinds. She hated people looking in on their business. At eight o'clock a timer would turn on the Christmas lights strewn around the banksia tree on the front lawn. Neither Luke nor Trace said anything. They had heard the 'sacrifices' talk before. It was as tired and worn as their parents' marriage.

'Look,' their dad said, glancing over at Luke, 'you're at uni with your books, trying to make a go of it ... That's more than we got when we were your age.'

Luke knew what 'making a go of it' meant. Both his parents worked at the cannery – even retail was a step up in their eyes.

'Don't see why he needs to go to university. Plenty of perfectly good jobs down at the mall,' his mother chimed in, her rosacea flushing as she twisted the top off a new bottle.

'We're talking about Trace,' Luke reminded her. His mother always deflected when it came to his sister.

Trace's face was distant, as if she hadn't heard a thing they'd said. After a moment's silence, she raised her can and said, 'Well, here's to your new grandchild and your niece or nephew.' She looked pointedly at Luke and added, 'By the way, I'm moving out.'

*

At home the lawn is overgrown, and he wonders if his parents have been waiting for him to come back and cut it. His bedroom has been taken over by storage boxes, Camping Australia map books and his dad's titty mags from the seventies. He flops onto his bed and a cloud of dust escapes beneath his old R2-D2 and C-3PO doona. He knows he'll spend the night wheezing. He flips through old magazines until he is sleepy.

When he wakes in the morning, his parents have already left for the cannery. He pulls on his old hiking gear, khaki shorts, thick socks and boots and grabs his inhaler. He makes coffee in the kitchen, looking for a thermos as the kettle boils. He is going to hit the trails on the old prospectors' hills up near the hospital. He sets off, trampling the front lawn with his boots, kicking the front gate open.

As a teenager, he was acutely aware of how close he was to this unbridled wilderness. The bush was an escape from the house, his mum and dad, from Trace and her skanky friends. Girls who wanted their cherries popped so bad, like a scab that needed picking off and couldn't be left alone. Trace had a whole lot of them lined up. One time four of them grabbed him, pinned him down, sticking their tongues down his throat, tugging at his pants before he pushed them off. 'You think you'd be grateful,' Trace had said. 'How else are you ever going to get laid?'

Behind the hospital car park is a pebbly dirt track that leads to the reserve. His coffee swooshes in the thermos in his backpack as he crunches stones underfoot. Either side of the track, rosellas and galahs are busy with their beaks in the dewy grass. After a hundred metres or so he turns around and can no longer see the car park; the entrance has closed over. Only the statue on top of the hospital is visible, Our Mother of Mercy with her hands clasped against the sky. He swings his arms and does a few shoulder rolls to loosen up, staring at the canopy. The sun is warm but not too hot yet, he might do six kilometres. The trails are uneven but well used by dirt-bike riders and cross-country runners. The ground is littered with gum leaves, kangaroo droppings and rubbish – crushed Coke cans, a used condom, chip wrappers fluttering about like confetti, an open Domino's Pizza box licked clean by possums. But if he keeps his eyes on the sky, he sees none of this. All he can hear are wattlebirds calling, his boots, the thermos swishing. He does this every morning he is home, before visiting hours start at the hospital.

*

He is here to support Trace. That is what he is told. He and his parents are pulled into one of the hospital's 'quiet rooms', where family members can stay overnight if they need to. They sit on gingham lounges with broken springs. A nurse stands before them. She has a long blonde ponytail that reaches her behind. Around her neck are several lanyards with keys and swipe cards dangling off them. Her name is Kirsty.

Luke remembers this quiet room, or one like it, from when his grandma died. They spent so much time sitting around as they waited for cancer to rob her of her last breath. He doesn't remember for how long but it had seemed important, the vigil, all of them together. Before his gran slipped into a coma, she asked for her jewellery box and handed out the contents. Tracey grabbed as much as she could. Their gran, loopy on morphine, offered jewellery to the nurses as well. His mum stood back and watched, nibbling at her nails. 'It's all junk, costume jewellery. She pawned the good stuff years ago,' she said.

She is chewing her nails now, listening to Kirsty. It is like an intervention. They need to be a united front.

'She needs to feel the love and encouragement of her family to move forward in the right direction when she is discharged,' Kirsty says, smiling at them.

'We didn't know. We didn't even know ...' his mother keeps muttering.

Kirsty says something about Trace being a high-functioning user. His mum and dad will come straight from work to the hospital each day, but for the rest of the time Luke is meant to stick around.

'Keep an eye on who comes to see her, keep the undesirables out,' his dad says under his breath.

*

When Tracey is showering or sleeping – they give her sleeping pills so she won't writhe all the time, scratching her arms till they bleed – Luke goes to the special care nursery to see his nephew. Tracey named him PJ for reasons that were beyond him. The nursery is dimly lit and he peers through the glass at the screaming babies, their rigid arms thrusting out from their bodies. Their little feet offering sharp kicks to the air. Some are shuddering like when you dream you're falling, slipping through your bed and there's nothing below.

'It's called the startle reflex. It's more pronounced in babies who had prenatal substance exposure,' Kirsty told him the other day. She had been blowing on a cup of herbal tea in the canteen while he lined up for coffee.

His nephew's dark hair is plastered to his purple, waxy forehead, his fists clenched. Kirsty swaddles him till he is tightly cocooned in a bolt of muslin. He has watched her re-swaddle him about twenty times already; the moment she puts him down he thrashes about violently. Luke worries that one day he will buck himself out of the crib, flipping over the plastic barrier and landing flat on his little purple face.

Don't put him down, he wants to call through the glass. But there were four other babies doing the exact same thing. Kirsty wraps each of them in turn, holding them upright against her chest, pacing the length of the room, patting their bottoms, shushing. They shriek the whole time but she never cocks her ear away, just keeps on pacing with small, even steps, her ponytail swishing back and forth.

'He's got a good pair of lungs,' his mum says, sidling up to him at the window. She has finished work so he is officially off duty. He can go home and hit the books; he has essays to write and has missed a load of lectures.

'He'll be a sprinter like our Trace. Stawell Gift for that one, I reckon,' his mum adds, nodding at her reflection in the glass as if to reinforce her statement.

He stays silent, wanting no part of this, pretending what this kid's future might be like. He wonders how long he has to stick around for.

*

His sister had been a runner. A good one. She was always the fastest girl in her age group. She had muscular, spindly legs that ran as well across long distances as they did short. She often beat much older kids, even boys. One year in high school at cross-country she challenged the seniors as they gathered at the start line.

'I'm going to beat youse all and I'm going to do it with no shoes,' she said as she pulled off her Dunlop Volleys and hurled them into the bush. There was much whooping and laughing, and some of the boys wolf-whistled. 'On ya, Trace,' they called. Girls twittered and jeered. Mr Woodley, the PE teacher, kept quiet but had a smug look on his face before he blew the whistle. They took off in a pack until the fastest few broke forward into single file. Luke dawdled behind with the other asthmatics, a boy with cerebral palsy and the teacher assigned to the back of the pack to check for cheaters or those stopping to smoke.

Tracey won, of course. She even beat the fastest guy in Year 12. Her feet were coated in fine, orange dirt. Her soles were bleeding, skin flayed, toenails torn asunder. She was a legend that day. Everyone thought they knew what future path awaited her.

*

His days have a new rhythm to them. He walks every morning in the bush, listening to birds calling and the drilling sound of cicadas. The same battered cross-country route they used at school. He never does this in Sydney. There is no bush at Sydney Uni. He doesn't exercise at all there; he stays indoors – lecture halls, tuition rooms, the library, his flat, bars. Since he's been back, even though he sets out early, his skin has become tinged with pink. He's got more vitamin D in a few days than during the whole semester. After his walk, he heads to the hospital. He watches reruns of *Wheel of Fortune* with Trace in her room. The TV is bolted to the ceiling and costs seven dollars per day to rent. His mum complains it's highway robbery, every time she walks in the room.

'I always wanted to go on this show,' Trace says.

'As a contestant?' he asks, wondering if she meant as Adriana, the hostess, gliding back and forth in '80s couture as she turned the white tiles to reveal the missing letters.

'Yes,' she says, before suddenly screaming, 'MICROWAVE!' at the TV, guessing the word from only one letter. A nurse checking the blood pressure of another patient glares at them.

He prefers to spend time outside the special care nursery. If Kirsty is on duty she pops her head out and talks to him. He likes that. She told him PJ looks like him. They still have no idea who the father is. Whoever he is, he hasn't come to the hospital. Neither have any of Trace's friends who hang out at the Boomerang Hotel. This surprises Trace. 'Bitches,' she called them. 'Don't even want to meet my new baby,' she complained to Luke. He isn't surprised; her friends were off their faces, leading the life that Tracey is supposed to be trying to avoid. He suspects as soon as she gets out she will fall in with them again.

'I want the baby taken away from her and given to social services,' he tells Kirsty one afternoon.

Kirsty, her expression warm and open without judgement, places a hand on his arm.

'We can't forcibly remove him from his mother when he's not in any danger. Tracey is undergoing treatment, she is cooperative. She would have to sign forms. I don't think she'd want to do that,' she says.

'No, she wants the parenting allowance,' he replies.

Kirsty tells him the best place for PJ is with his mother with the support of his grandparents and a doting uncle.

Sometimes when he can't sleep, he gets up and rummages through the boxes in his room. He finds Tracey's old medals and the plastic ornamental jewellery tree his mother used to hang them on. 'Chalk and cheese, those two,' his mother told the neighbours when they were young, or anyone else who would listen. 'That one,' she'd point to Luke, 'been reading since he came out of the womb.'

But it was Trace she liked to talk about. As he puts the medals back in the box, he thinks of his mum getting up early all those Saturday mornings for Little Athletics. Sitting on the sidelines with a clunky old stopwatch, while he read a book in the grandstand. He places the cheap jewellery tree back on top of the medals. It had always looked tacky.

*

Tracey lost a race once. It was one of those novelty races they have at kids' sports carnivals, the fun part of the day where parents race the teachers and get all hot and bothered. Overweight dads keel over at the finish line, panting like they have blown a gasket. Kids line up for sack races and the egg and spoon. Normally Luke never competed because of his asthma, but a teacher, Miss O'Keefe, pushed him to join in. She partnered him with Tracey for the three-legged race because they were the same height. She stood them side by side and bound their legs with a rainbow ribbon above the knees. He looped his arm around Tracey's skinny waist.

'We're going to lose,' Luke whispered, imagining what Tracey's fist would feel like when it connected with his rib cage.

'It's okay. Just keep walking so we don't trip,' she whispered back. 'Just keep walking.'

He nodded and as other kids tumbled over, or got disqualified when their ribbons broke apart, he and Tracey walked in a straight line to the finish. Their sides were pressed together like when they were in the womb. They came third. It was the nicest thing his sister had ever done for him.

*

The semester will be over soon and PJ and Trace are still in the hospital. Luke emailed essays to his lecturers and skimmed a bunch of lecture videos online. He transferred rent money to his flatmates with specific instructions not to sublet his room. It's nearly summer and he's been waking earlier for his walks to beat the heat. He often now passes his mum in the hallway as she gets ready for work, or sees his dad peeing with the bathroom door open.

This morning the sky is dark violet, the sun not fully up. There is enough light to see the trails but the nocturnal animals are still awake. Fruit bats peer at him, upside down in the trees. He can hear a rooster crowing from someone's backyard in the distance. A wallaby skitters in the scrub, startled by the crunch of his boots. He stops suddenly when he spots the amber eyes of a large owl. It's resting on a low branch. As he walks closer, he sees a sugar glider in its talons. Its head ripped off, the owl's powerful beak tearing at flesh, the wing-like flaps hanging in tatters.

As Luke walks away, queasy, he remembers something, another time he was up early, nearly colliding with his mum in the hallway. He was a teenager, he'd woken up to go to the bathroom, and his mum was bustling into Tracey's room with an arm full of toiletries. Tracey was on her bed in a tracksuit, looking glum, knees tucked up under her chin. His mum was packing a bag. He spoke to them for a few minutes, yawning in his boxer shorts. He'd thought maybe Trace was going to the track but normally she was up like a bolt for training. His mum was talking quietly; she didn't want to wake their father. She told him Tracey was going to hospital for the day, she was having trouble with her periods, needed a curette. Luke headed back to bed.

That night, their mum charred the chops as usual. They ate them with withered beans and mash potato the colour of margarine. The TV was propped on the kitchen counter, facing the dining table. His parents' eyes would flick to the local news, commenting if they saw someone they knew, tut-tutting about local crime and waiting with bated breath for the weather report. Normally, Luke would look at Trace and roll his eyes, but that day she wasn't looking back. That day had been like any other except it wasn't. Something was erased. The spark went out of Trace's eyes and then she lost interest in running altogether.

*

In the afternoon, Luke wheels a pram all the way from Main Street to the hospital. In a few days, Tracey and PJ can leave. Trace agreed to move back in with their mum and dad. Kirsty had given his parents a list of stuff babies need but there seemed to be confusion about who was getting what. His parents were getting a car seat fitted at the RTA, but he knew no one had thought to buy a pram. When he saw it in the window of St Vincent De Paul, he thought it charming, sturdy, vintage. He imagined his little nephew reclining, relaxed, nestled in muslin, shielded from the sun by the PVC concertina cover.

'You've got to be kidding me,' Trace says when he wheels the pram into her room. She is sitting in bed, fully dressed. She no longer wears the hospital gowns and is back to her normal attire, gym pants and a cropped singlet showing her midriff, which she never stopped wearing even when she was no longer sporty.

'PJ needs a pram so you can take him out and stuff, wheel him around,' Luke says.

'He's going to be a laughing stock in that thing. Looks like it's from the olden days!' She laughs. 'How do you even fold it?' She gets up and walks around it, tapping the wheels with her toe.

That's a good point, he thinks, realising he doesn't know. Tracey tells him new prams collapse to about the size of a carry-on suitcase, so they fit in the boot of your car with your shopping. This pram is tall and boxy, more like a cot on wheels with a sunroof. He begins looking around for a button or lever that would make the whole thing fall in a heap. The wheels are as large as those on a toddler's bike. He had been taken in by the shiny spokes buffed with Brasso by some volunteer at Vinnies, by the thick rubber wheels and their all-terrain tread.

'Fucking useless,' Trace says, shaking her head. He doesn't know if she means him or the pram. He feels his neck flush red, his pulse throbbing at his temples.

'Well, you can give me a hand,' he says, inspecting a lever, possibly a brake pedal that looks rusted into place.

Tracey walks around slowly, hands on her hips, staring at the pram. He squats by the wheels, level with her navel. Despite giving birth her stomach is practically concave and all of a sudden he wants to punch that smooth, hollow space.

'Where are the instructions?' she asks.

'There are none, it's second-hand. Vintage,' he snaps.

She scoffs, running her hand along the handles. She opens and closes the sun cover four times – just to annoy him, he thinks – each stiff, dividing panel needs a tug and a push to fold and unfold it. The lever by the wheel is surely part of the mechanism that collapses the pram, but he needs WD-40 to shift it. He begins to regret buying it.

'What if we can't close it? Or we close it and we can't open it again?' he asks, his chest tightening. If the pram can't fit in their parents' car, it won't be going anywhere. He looks at it with a new sense of distrust. Tracey shrugs and pulls out the interior mattress, goodness knows why.

'Tracey, I'm serious.' He looks up at her. He shouldn't have bought the bloody thing. *If we can't even open and close a pram, what kind of future will PJ have?* he thinks. He lets his fingers rest on the rusted pedal. Sitting on the pine-fresh floor beside Tracey's bed, he feels he could just crawl under there and take a rest. It was so hot walking all the way from Main Street uphill to the hospital.

Tracey is standing above him, one hand on the handle, when she raises her leg. Her bare, cool foot slams down on her brother's hand with force. The ancient pram folds forward in three slow movements and he scrambles to get his hand out of the way. His fingers throb. Tracey is grinning, resting one foot on top of the collapsed hood like it's a podium she's about to mount.

*

Kirsty is waiting for him outside the nursery, a smile on her face. This might be the last time he sees her. He is heading back to Sydney for his exams and a summer job.

'It's time for PJ to go outside,' she says, grabbing his hand and pulling him into the nursery.

'What do you mean?' he asks.

'I mean fresh air. He's strong enough. Let's take him for a lap of the hospital garden.' She walks over to PJ's crib and picks him up, nodding to another nurse on duty.

'Great. I'll go get Trace and the pram,' he says. Kirsty pauses and lowers her gaze, playing with the muslin around his nephew in her arms.

'Yes, of course.' There is a small frown on her brow and she seems embarrassed. He realises then what this is: a moment alone, a chance for the three of them to say goodbye. He has spent so many hours on the other side of the glass, watching Kirsty and PJ. He didn't think PJ would ever know he was there but Kirsty knew; every day he'd spoken to her a little. He decides to change tack before it's too late and reaches for her arm as she lowers PJ back into the crib.

'Actually, I think Trace has NA now anyway. I'd love to. Let's go,' he says.

They ride the elevator together to the ground floor. PJ is cradled against Kirsty, his arms and legs scrunched up in swaddling.

Luke glances in the elevator mirrors at Kirsty's long ponytail from three different angles. She is a bit older than him, maybe three or four years. He wonders what would happen if she lived in Sydney, or if he lived here. Every now and then PJ sighs, chirps, hiccups, makes the noises of a normal baby.

The hospital's automatic doors swing open and they are outside. PJ blinks in the bright light. Sparrows flit about on the grass and two magpies splash in a birdbath. There is a warm breeze and PJ's lips pucker at the wind. Kirsty passes the baby to Luke. *He's as light as a loaf of bread*, Luke thinks. He looks down at this creature that shares his DNA and hopes PJ gets his hair and brains. Kirsty loops her arm through his as they walk in small, even steps in the sunlight. The picture of a normal family. As they near the hospital gates he feels an overwhelming urge to pass through them – that at this moment anything is possible, that everything will be perfect if he just keeps walking.

One's Company

Elizabeth Flux

As they stepped off the plane, Zhen's mother turned to hold his hand and was met with two different versions of her son. She *tsk'd* impatiently. There were bags to collect and paperwork to fill out – she didn't have time for magical realism.

Grabbing each one of them by the hand as they made their way down the rickety stairs she sighed in the language of what used to be home.

'Pull yourself together,' she said. Sheepishly, the New One disappeared, and Zhen was one person again.

He waited patiently as the customs man dug through his mother's suitcase, taking things out one by one and peering at them intently. Looking in one plastic bag, the man's eyes briefly lit up before disappointment settled in; he'd discovered air-travel-approved packets of tea, and not the dried fruit or meat he was expecting. A fair-haired man casually tossed down his bag at the next table, and the woman barely unzipped the top before waving him along. The customs man moved on to their rice cooker. With his blue uniform and gold badge he looked like the policeman from the comics about famous Australians they'd handed out to the children on the plane. Zhen saw his mother flinch but say nothing as the rice cooker was roughly reassembled before they were let on their way with a small grunt and a hollow 'Enjoy your visit'.

'Oh we are here to stay,' laughed his mother, locking eyes with the customs man.

'Right,' he said dismissively, signalling to the next in line.

She shooed Zhen forwards and they hurriedly made their way out of the airport, past the smiling posters of blonde families having beach picnics. He carried a stuffed black bear, which was almost as big as he was, and as he held it, paw to hand, scurrying after his mother, he tried to imagine himself and Bear in the place of the posed couple, trapped forever clinking wine glasses against an ocean backdrop.

*

On his first day at the new school his shoes were wrong. Lined up outside the classroom, Zhen's sneakers stood out immediately against the sea of white. 'Too colourful,' said the note sent home from his teachers. 'And uniform policy prefers laces over Velcro.' At roll call they'd gingerly announced his last name, getting confused by the unfamiliar order and mixture of letters.

'John,' he corrected, giving the name he'd picked from the small list his parents had come up with. It was in this extra time that his teacher noticed the shoes.

'Right,' she said dubiously.

His parents debated whether or not it was worth buying him a second pair, and decided not to. It was impractical.

'He'll grow out of them in six months,' his father said. Zhen split in two again, and his new self kicked out at the offending sneakers.

'There's no call for that,' his father said. 'And what has your mother told you about this double act you keep pulling?' Zhen, sitting on the couch, raised his palms apologetically. His other, silent self scowled and disappeared again. His parents switched on the news and Zhen sat quietly, poring over the small comic book, trying to memorise the story of Monga and his own adjustment to their shared adopted home.

He'd already read it cover to cover, but kept coming back to the same three pages, the same face. Monga didn't look like anyone from home, but he didn't look like any of the people from their new street either. Zhen was enthralled. His parents wouldn't let him take the comic to school – *how will you learn if you just read the same thing over and over?* – so he'd painstakingly drawn

Monga's face twice: one on the toes of each of his sneakers.

The other children were fascinated, but it became frustrating to try to explain who the character was. When he told them he was Australian, they scoffed and when he said the man's name was Monga, the other children squealed with laughter.

'MONG-a?' exclaimed his classmate Cody. 'You drew a mong on your shoes?'

'Makes sense,' chimed in Lachy, pulling at the corner of his eyes. 'Mongs drawing mongs.'

The nickname stuck.

*

Before school had started for the year, his parents received a booklist and some suggestions for what their child would need, day to day.

Sandshoes for P.E. and for going in the sandpit.

A fruit box for recess.

Something for Show 'n' Tell.

They were an English-speaking household though Zhen and his mother were bilingual. Ten years too early for the internet and yet to make friends on their street, his father tried turning to the surprisingly unhelpful dictionary.

At recess Zhen opened his lunch box full of carefully sliced peaches, banana and canned longan while the other children plunged straws into tetrapacks, slurping aggressively, speedily – racing.

'What's that, Mong?' demanded Cody.

'My fruit box?' replied Zhen, after a pause.

The hoots of laughter and streams of mocking gibberish followed him as he trudged towards the empty corner of the sandpit and flopped down, alone.

Mou mo! Wu zhou lat tat! Don't touch it! It's dirty! cried his mother at the back of his mind.

The ghost of her advice was right; the sand was probably teeming with germs, but he gingerly started digging one foot in, then the other, and soon was grabbing fistfuls and heaping them on top of his shoes. Half sunk in, the colour and Monga's face soon got buried by the most gentle of avalanches.

*

In the comic, Monga was just one of many going about his life against the background that Zhen had been told was the Real Australia. There were sparkling oceans, there were giant fields – and there were stretches of sand, the soft yellows and oranges making a false sea more expansive than anything he'd ever witnessed. Missing were the tall towers of home, the streets packed with people. Every Saturday morning he could remember, Ah Poh would come collect him and they'd navigate the market together. His grandmother was ruthless in her bargaining, rapidly firing off the list of what she wanted to buy along with the price she expected to pay, their shared monosyllabic language making conversation sound like rapid linguistic gunfire.

Their new home was slower; people savoured sounds like John savoured the lychees Ah Poh would unshell and pop in his mouth to keep him from complaining when their trips went for just a little too long. The shops here were different; clean, quiet. There were no crates leaking melted ice and fish scales onto a slippery floor. People didn't talk, they just walked up and down in straight lines, stacking plastic and cardboard on top of each other in their trolleys.

*

Monga disappeared into the sand completely and the bell rang. Zhen felt himself split in two again, but this time there was no one to tell him off.

The New One stood up and followed his classmates into the schoolroom. Zhen stayed in the sand, and contemplated his shoes.

*

Over the following weeks Zhen was sometimes singular and sometimes plural – something which frustrated his parents and teachers alike. His father grumbled as he was forced, yet again, to inflate their blow-up mattress to accommodate 'this silliness'. The New One merely grinned and played with his Tazos. Zhen ignored him. Another firmly polite letter had come home with him after the teachers finally noticed the drawings, and he was now tracing out Monga again, this time on the soles of his new, stark-white sneakers so no one would see.

He sat, or sometimes they'd sit, every Wednesday as his class rotated through their turns for show-and-tell. There were pine-cones and older brothers' trophies, VHS tapes of Disney cartoons, or ticket stubs from that weekend's football. When Zhen raised his hand to ask why the ball a classmate had brought in was long instead of round, The New One flushed and shuffled further away.

When his week came, Zhen didn't even need to think about it. He carefully packed the comic between two exercise books so it wouldn't bend in his bag and, arriving at the classroom, slipped his backpack in the usual spot: above his name tag, which the teacher had cheerfully decorated with a wombat sticker, between Hannah (emu) and Lachy (bilby).

Zhen was more excited than he had been all year; he was still 'Mong' to most of his classmates, who seemed to have forgotten where they'd gotten the name to begin with. He'd kept quiet about the secret drawings that were slowly wearing away as he trudged from class to class, and from running around in the occasional game of chasey he would join in on – when asked.

'I brought my comic,' he told his table, sitting down before roll call.

'It's in my bag. You can all see it after lunch.' Cody, who sat opposite, looked at him.

'Why? We won't be able to read it.'

Zhen stared briefly at Cody, before muscle memory brought his gaze back down to the desk – but he could still see the boy pull-ing up at the corners of his own eyes, making gibberish noises as the rest of the table giggled. He felt the split happen again, and The New One joined in, a beat after the others. Zhen stayed quiet, eyes fixed on the table, grinding his left shoe into the linoleum.

The other children were mostly uninterested in Zhen. He didn't impress them at sport, and wasn't the best at any of the other things that seemed important: drawing the straightest lines or having the most stickers on the book chart. He knew the alphabet but had sung different songs at his kindergarten back home, so didn't know as many lyrics to the songs they'd sing each morning. On the occasions they did pay attention, it was usually to point out something he was doing wrong: tying laces with one loop instead of bunny ears; pronouncing words differently; not knowing the difference between dress and skirt.

At lunchtime Zhen retreated to his usual patch of grass. He'd just plunged the spoon into his thermos when two girls from his table ran up, halfway between upset and laughing. 'Cody's reading your comic,' one of them said, with a giggle at the end. 'Thought you should know.' They retreated, Zhen's eyes following them, then overtaking, looking over at the backpack shelf where he could see Cody and some friends crouched over something.

They'd gone by the time Zhen got to his bag, which was unzipped. The comic was shoved roughly in at the top, no longer protected by the exercise books. Every page was crumpled, some ripped in half. The New One walked into the classroom and sat alone at his desk, slowly running his fingers over the damaged pages. Zhen stayed at his bag, quietly looking down at his ruined book, before clenching his fists and moving in the direction of Cody.

*

Zhen remained plural.

*

It was okay at first. When it became apparent that the split was permanent, his father begrudgingly bought a second bed. To avoid confusion the family decided to call The New One John. John and Zhen started out quite alike, doing the same after-hours activities and speaking the language that no one else understood when they wanted to discuss things in secret during class. The line down the middle of their room began to appear slowly; Zhen's side filling up with certificates proclaiming his aptitude for maths and science, John's with sporting trophies and CDs.

'You boys are being a bit literal,' scolded their father as Zhen quietly ate fish with his parents while John sat in the other room, fuming that he wasn't allowed to go to the sleepover that clashed with the festival no one else was celebrating.

*

They sat, side by side, in the middle of the night, in the house where they'd lived for almost ten years, eyes fixed on the television – watching the two towers fall after a frantic call from Ah Poh. Their mother came home from work the next day and quietly recounted how a colleague had asked her if she'd 'heard the news'.

'Yes. We watched while it happened,' she'd replied.

'Isn't it awful,' said the woman. 'But your lot's okay.'

Zhen's face tightened, while next to him, John seemed not to have heard, too engrossed in the Paul Jennings book he'd gotten out from the library.

*

Once a month, their mother would call Ah Poh. After discussing their health complaints and listing the meals they'd eaten that day, Ah Poh would scold her daughter for letting Zhen split into two separate people, blaming both diet and the fact that she wasn't at home enough. Then the phone would be handed to the boys to answer questions about how school was going; if they were eating enough; when they would be coming to visit. At the beginning John and Zhen would take turns answering. Eventually, though, it got to the point where John would make excuses – homework, tiredness, anything – to avoid talking on the phone, and Zhen and Ah Poh would be left alone, rattling off friendly fire.

Over time, the phone calls got fewer and further between. Even so, it took Zhen a surprisingly long time to realise that people had stopped seeing him altogether; it took him even longer to realise that it was John who had done this to him. He came home from school one day to see that his bed had been packed up and put in the garage. As he turned to go back in the house, his hand passed right through the doorknob.

John refused to give him an explanation. He screamed and shouted and begged, but his corporeal self pretended not to hear. Zhen sunk to the ground, and found himself dragged along in John's wake, an invisible wall forbidding him to get more than ten metres away.

'Uggh, shut up, Mong,' was the most he got out of John in six months of solitude. He couldn't remember what the original Monga looked like; the crumpled book was still squeezed in on his shelf, but you can't turn pages with faded hands.

*

It took a few years, but Zhen got used to the silence. He lay dormant, watching himself reply to his mother's home-tongue questions in English, watching himself refuse to take leftovers to school anymore.

He watched as the calligraphy set from Ah Poh got dusty, got moved behind the trophies and eventually found a home at the back of a cupboard, the wax seal on the ink never breaking, as the liquid slowly dehydrated, turning to residue; unusable.

He filled the long lonely stretches by drawing invisible pictures; his bedroom became the market as he traced his finger along the wall, creating crates and cages and characters who existed even less than he did, disappearing centimetre by centimetre in his wake. The times he felt seen were few, and he didn't know if they were just the product of a desperate hope.

In their monthly phone call Ah Poh congratulated John's mother on finally getting him past his phase, though, when the phone was handed to John, her disappointment at hearing *dui mm zhi, mm ming bak* more than anything else was readily apparent.

'Put me on the phone,' begged Zhen. 'I can help.'

Zhoi gein. Goodbye. See you again. John hung up the phone.

*

It was university holidays and Zhen watched as his friends who'd never met him sat around a table, growing hazier with each round of the drinking game they were yet to grow tired of. A circle of cards surrounded a jug filled with a mixture of drinks and he saw himself pull an ace.

'RULE!' the group shrieked as one. But they were stumped; awash with power and dulled by alcohol, they were at a loss as to how to wield it. There was silence.

A boy with slightly darker skin than the rest stole a sideways glance at John as he sat, running his index finger along the edge of the card, waiting.

'I know,' he said with a grin. 'We all have to speak in our first language. Or drink.'

Zhen found himself sitting in John's place, the card now in his hand. People were *looking* at him. He burbled out a sentence in his long silent voice, perfectly pronounced. His friends laughed, and continued drawing cards. Zhen smiled, and behind him, in the corner, John was furious. When the final king was pulled, ending the game, the rumble switched them back and both sat in sullen silence: one filled with anger, the other hollowed out.

*

Ah Poh's visit came at the worst possible time – in that period between exams finishing and getting results back. John was nervous, worried about failure in a year where the absence of school's structure had exposed his laziness.

'Vi-sit,' he'd intoned during their phone call.

'Fisit,' she'd shot back. 'Fisit?' The language they'd once shared had no call for the letter V.

Hou loi mei gein.

John sat alongside himself in the back of the car, watching Zhen's knee bounce up and down as he gazed out the window. Their father found a park close to the entrance and they all clambered out. They saw the poster at the same time. Out of the corner of his eye, John could see Zhen looking down at the memory of colourful shoes, long since thrown away, then back up again, comparing. He blinked, turning away from Zhen, then stared straight ahead at the face he hadn't seen since he'd wedged the crumpled comic in between two thick books, wincing as his bruised knuckles touched against the spines.

Dui mm ji, he said, the words stiff, formal and unheard.

I'm sorry, he said, to himself, and to no one.

By Proxy

Cassie Hamer

It is Rosa's last night on the MV *Toscana*, and she would quite like to die. The boiling sea has muddled her insides. Stomach in mouth. Heart in knees. The cabin is stifling and the vessel is in delirium, pickled by sea salt and alcohol.

Above her, from the dining hall, the piano accordion wheezes and gasps a slurred tune. Heels and toes keep syncopated time on the wooden floorboards. Below her, the bunk vibrates as the ship's engines power and shudder through the swell.

'Rosa! Rosa! *Vieni alla festa. Adesso!' Rosa, come to the party. Now!* Through the keyhole slides Maria's voice, lubricated by alcohol and hoary with cigarettes.

But Rosa does not want to go to the party. She wants to die. She wants Mama to smooth the hair on her forehead and bring her stale ciabatta and *aqua minerale*. She does not want to be this message in a bottle, at the mercy of tides and currents.

'No. *Sto male.' I'm sick.* Rosa rolls with the ship and her stomach heaves in time with both. Tomorrow night, he will be in her bed. Mama has said it will hurt, but she is not to cry. The blood will please him.

Her stomach reels again.

'*Va bene*, Rosa.' *Okay.* From the unsteady beat of Maria's foot-steps, Rosa knows she is stumbling down the hallway, lurching from side to side.

For Rosa, sleep is a butterfly beyond reach. Instead, she practises her English. Like a baby trying new fruit, she lolls her tongue around the foreign words, tasting and testing them and swallowing the sound in her throat.

'My name is Rosa. How you do? What your name is?'

The words are a lullaby, talking her to sleep. In her dreams, the white caps are the ghostly fingers of souls lost at sea, grasping at the resolute little boat and trying to pull it under to join them in eternal rest.

*

It is the silence that wakes her. Are they still sailing? Rosa shimmies out of the bunk, past Maria's pale and snoring face. The girl is nocturnal. For all the passengers, the voyage has been dream-like for its strange configuration of people and behaviours. On this boat, they are not themselves. There is no cooking, no cleaning, no work. They are between lives. Adrift.

Sitting on her trunk, Rosa pulls on the silk stockings she has been saving. The rest of her trousseau is stowed safely in the hold. There is Mama's porcelain dining set, the lace tablecloth that comes out at Christmas, and napkins Mama used for her wedding day. All that is new is a chemise, for later, and the stockings. Word on the boat is that one of the English ladies has nylons, but she has a cabin on the upper deck and it is only a rumour.

In the bathroom Rosa pinches her cheeks for colour. Maria has promised to loan her some rouge but there is no thought of waking her now. She adjusts the wool duster coat, the same one she wore for the photo she sent him. The one of him is in her pocket. She doesn't need to look, for his face appears whenever she closes her eyes, pushing through the greeny-redness. She touches the picture, though. Rubs it like a talisman. The surface is even smoother than the silk lining of her pocket. She repeats the words Mama said: 'Good hair. White teeth. Not too skinny. A good man.'

Hopefully, he has not changed. She remembers him a little from childhood. Hide-and-seek in the olive trees with all the other kids of the village. But that was before the war, before all the men went off to fight and his family moved south to be with his aunt and cousins.

Up on deck, the morning is blue velvet. The ship leaves a cat-
erpillar trail of smoke. A deckhand is clearing the streamers
from last night's party but stops when he sees her. He leans on
his broom and points to the water.

'Derwent ... Derwent.' She repeats after him, 'Derwent.' But
perhaps her pronunciation is no good, for the young man shakes
his head at her and resumes sweeping.

As the sun arcs into the sky, the ship's occupants emerge slowly
onto the deck – blinking like pipis brought to the sand's surface.
The river is wide and blue but the land is flat and unimpressively
empty and disappointment ripples through the crowd.

They were expecting paradise.

With a gentle bump against the pier, the ship delivers Rosa
into her new life. The dock is curiously deserted. No streamers.
No band. Here, they are not known. There is no family. They are
new and friendless.

He is easy to spot. Dark eyes flitting across the deck before
they come to rest on her. He's slimmer than in the photo.

Through a scudding heartbeat, she smiles. He gives a half-
hearted wave in return, his hand dropping quickly as Maria, now
standing beside Rosa and smelling of musty wine, starts blowing
kisses.

'*Smettila!*' *Stop it!* Rosa hisses.

'What? It's my husband.'

It is then Rosa notices the other dark-haired man running
down the pier and waving his cap. The husband Maria has not
seen in two years.

'*Cara, mio. Cara, mio!*' *My darling, my darling!* he shouts.

Tears have streaked Maria's rouge. Her smile is tight.

Does she cry for what has been, or what is to come?

Rosa is suddenly aware of an ache in her finger where the cool
breeze has settled on the silver of her wedding band. It is slightly
too small but he has promised a new one for the ceremony
tomorrow, before they leave Hobart for the hydro. There will be
a priest and one family member, a cousin who works with him.

'You do this for the children,' said Mama. 'They will want the
photo.'

Her wedding dress is in the trunk, wrapped around the dinner setting. Her veil just fitted inside the tureen. There is a small

red wine stain on the hem where Papa was too excited. It is not every day your daughter marries, even if the groom is half a world away! But she thinks her husband will not notice the mark.

The gangplank is lowering.

'Rosa, *in bocca a lupo.*' Rosa, *good luck! Into the mouth of the wolf.* Maria will be living in Hobart, and the hydro is two hours away. Rosa does not expect to see her again.

The pair embrace. '*Crepi il lupo*, Maria.' *And to you*, Maria. *May the wolf croak.*

With her bouncing stride, Maria makes the plank wobble to the point where Rosa must cling to the handrail. Her palms are greasy. Clicking heels will be the last she sees of the older girl.

For the first time in weeks, Rosa steps onto dry land. She sways from the firmness. The solidity. She is not used to such steadiness and he rushes to take her hand.

'I've got you' are the first words she hears from her husband's mouth, as she stumbles before straightening.

She drops his hand. 'I'm sorry.'

The apology is shrugged away. 'Is this all?' He gestures to the small trunk in her hand.

'No, there is another coming. The trousseau.'

The crew is starting to unload the hold and Rosa and her husband stand together in silence until her case is placed alongside all the others.

Their hotel is not far and he decides they will walk.

'Battery Point.' He nods over the pier to a small piece of land jutting into the river. 'The government.' A sandstone building. 'Mount Wellington.' He lifts his eyes skyward.

'A mountain?' It is nothing like the ones at home, which are sharp-edged and snow-capped and graze the clouds. This one is squat and fat, with houses dotted into its protective foothills. A nonna, with grandchildren coddled into the folds of her dress.

As they walk, she is aware of his breathing, laboured by the strain of carrying two trunks. She has never listened so closely to a person's breath. The way it's catching in his throat as it constricts with effort. She supposes this is what it is to really notice someone, to be married.

Their room is up a slender set of stairs, above some kind of public bar. As he fumbles with the key, she is sure he must hear her heart beating. Will he want it now, or will they at least wait until the sun has set? When the door opens and he stands aside to let her through, she can barely walk and her teeth chatter out of control.

There are two beds. Narrow, but definitely separate. The one-foot gap between them may as well be an ocean and Rosa reaches for the wall to hold her up. He has not spoken since pointing out the bathroom on the landing.

'I have a letter from your mother,' says Rosa, and she starts busying herself with the trunks that he has placed in the corner. The bed creaks as he sits, frowning.

'She is well, and your father too. Your little brother has a cough but it is nothing to worry about.' She is babbling but cannot seem to stop. 'The summer has been terrible. All the village is suffering. There is no water for anything. Since the war, you know. You are so lucky—'

At that he sighs and Rosa falls silent. She concentrates on the clips, and curses herself. No one is lucky. But here they are, alive.

Finally, the lid of the trunk is free and she opens it to find great creamy swathes of fabric – the wedding dress she swaddled so carefully about the plates and the tureen. She digs in with archaeological purpose but instead of finding smooth porcelain, her fingers are met with hard, grainy edges that threaten to cut her skin. A vision of her trunk being tilled about by the ocean brings a wave of seasickness that Rosa tries to swallow away.

The first plate is broken in three. The second is in four pieces. The third is shattered as well. They all are. The trunk is littered with shards. She bows her head and coughs, shamed by her tears. But silently, he kneels beside her and together they begin to arrange the pieces on the floor. They could be children doing a jigsaw puzzle, but to Rosa they are grave robbers, picking through white bone.

In the trunk, there is one piece left. The tureen. To Rosa's surprise, it is intact. She splays her hands around the cool base of the round basin and cradles it with the care of a new mother.

'The letter is in here,' says Rosa. 'And my veil.'

He nods and she indicates for him to take it, which he does.

But the brush of fingertips is so unexpected, so warm, that Rosa lets go of the tureen and it falls to the ground with a great smash.

For a second, there is silence. Then there is a howl of despair and Rosa is shocked to discover that it is hers. What does it matter? There is nothing left now for her to lose.

She becomes aware of a hand on her shoulder. She looks at the man she does not know but is expected to love. Gently, he pulls her head towards his chest and smooths her hair as she sobs into him.

'Shhh,' he croons. 'We will make it right.'

And as she feels his heart, beating loud and strong, and sending blood to all corners of his body, she is inclined to believe him.

Sis Better

Ellen van Neerven

1.

Sis left her belt on the road, curled up like a king brown. She had just a singlet and grey jeans and one bag on her, no shoes.

She'd woken up to her name outside the bedroom window. Saw that it was a bird making the sound. The cockatoo called over and over again until there wasn't any doubt what was being said.

2.

The bus got her halfway to her grandfather's country. She said to herself, Sis better make good on this. It's the only thing that makes sense. Made more sense than ever.

The sun was hot on the pavement and many of the passengers went straight to the convenience store across the road. She took her bag out of the back and stood in front next to the timetable. A couple and their young son were a few metres away. She heard them talking. Folding the child's jacket into a small square, the man was travel-nervous, the woman was not. Looking down the row of shops and cafes, the woman was hungry, the man was not. Sis's ears were alert: the cockatoo had got her listening.

3.

She got in the couple's car next to the child strapped into a booster seat.

Is Paul Kelly okay? the man asked.

I'd prefer if you had his older stuff.

So you've come here to climb the mountain? the woman asked.

Not to climb. To see.

You're not climbing?

The elders forbid it.

There was another pause in the conversation.

Then the man gestured to the turn ahead. If you don't mind waiting, we're going to have lunch at the coast first.

She knew she didn't look like someone who could wait. She forced a smile, a thanks, to the mirror. She looked at the child. This child would be a white man.

The road bent through paperbarks, steered through banana plantations.

You gubs, she thought, I'm going to die on country. You will help me die.

The girl in the bakery was her cousin. Her uncle was working on the fire they passed on the freeway. She didn't look in their eyes.

4.

Sis had been asked to go in with the child because the parents didn't swim. She didn't want to be with them for any longer but held her patience thinking she needed the transport.

No surprises: no blacks on this beach or any non-whites. Massacre site. Many of the beaches here held that sort of history. Groups had been speared by the whites here, and a few beaches along, flour had been poisoned, killing another hundred local people. Wanted to tell the child when away from the parents. His mother took off his T-shirt and put the rash vest on him. Sis went in with her knickers and crop.

The water was colder than she remembered. The waves just right. The boy didn't want to go in until she told him he was a shark.

5.

Then of course the boy didn't want to get out when the mother called. He was having such a good time mixing up his encounter with waves, sometimes ducking under, sometimes flipping on his back, sometimes dunking himself on purpose, the saltwater and drool oozing out of his mouth. Sis was passive, watched until the mother, her yoga pants rolled up, walked in, her face scrunched up, and put her hand on the boy's shoulder. Told the boy his father was on his way to the pub and ordering chips.

On the way the woman was telling Sis and the boy that this park was named after her grandfather, the street after her uncle. Her grandfather's brother had built the pub, the maroon wooden building on the corner. A busy crew of people clustered above on the old balcony. Sis got herself a soda lime.

Eh, Sis! It was Donna, working behind the counter. You not drinking anymore?

Sis grabbed Donna's hand. Still working there, started when she was eighteen, maybe she was thirty-five-ish now. She was a skinny thing, James Baldwin book there next to the taps.

You okay there, Sis?

I'm okay. I'm happy to see you.

Coming tomorrow? I'm dancing.

You dancing with the troupe now?

Ceremony tomorrow at the cultural centre there.

The manager had come over, a tall older man. Bitch, I'm not paying you to talk to your rellos.

Donna glanced up at the people behind Sis. Men of the same type, waiting for beer.

Sis glared at the manager and didn't get out of the way.

He'd run out of patience. Fuck, it's not Abo o'clock.

Sis, enjoy your drink and being in town, Donna said calmly. Hope to catch up later. She winked at her.

Sis reluctantly walked away. The couple and their child had already finished their chips and were standing outside. They hadn't seen her and Donna together. She wanted them to go in there, to hear from Donna how many young people had topped themselves in this community just this year. Give them some sort of idea.

Daddy saw there's a storm coming, the child said as soon as she reached them.

A big one, he said. I'll get the car.

We should head home, the mother said.

Home was a fantasy. Long driveway down a dip. Cows in the paddock beside. Farmhouse with aircon and too many bathrooms. Nut trees and a cover of rain starting.

6.

Lightning rose like a flower. She would have never described it like this until tonight. This electrical storm had more strikes than she had ever seen: it just went on and on. It was enough to miss the light when it was not there, and she thought about how her mother, terrified of storms, had tried to give her this terror too but she had rejected it.

Her mind was quivering. They had put the four-year-old in with her, on the other bed, the child sleeping soundly. She couldn't not know the child was in there with her for a second so she had gone out in the hall to watch the storm – this is where she would sleep if she could sleep at all. She had promised her mind death on country when she got there, it was only just the valley below, down the hill.

Late that afternoon, when they came in off the coast road, they crossed the northern river and saw the mountain in the image and that's when she felt close.

She was moved to excitement. Twitching, wanting to wake the boy and show him how angry she was. Wanting to go into the couple's bedroom and tell them that this house wasn't meant to be here, that it was wrong that they were here.

She felt calm thinking of the taste of the grass on her lips as she found her final resting place back on country, on the foot of the mountain. How does the child sleep? Did he not hear the frogs? Wanting to die at the mountain to show she had been given life and she had given it back for Creation to give it to another.

She had not made nothing. Sis had made music – two records, more than twenty songs. Made two rooms out of one at her brother's place so her mum could live there and get away from their stepdad. Her mother missed country most. Missed it more than she did, until now. Her mother wanted to be back to the river, to their freshwater, to her family.

Her hands in little balls, her feet in falls – they kept sinking the rest of her with them. She saw a stranger walk towards her in a dream and then she shook awake again and the storm was still alive. She was still alive, though she could be broken by tears or breath or by her gut.

7.

She was nothing until morning, until the woman came to the breakfast bar and said the storm had killed two people on the summit of the mountain.

Two fellas, interstate tourists, had climbed, ignored lore. A tree had come down on them and they had been found in the morning.

Very sad, the woman said as a question.

I don't have words, Sis replied.

We slept right through it. The woman said. Could you sleep well?

I didn't sleep, I dreamt.

The coffee was perfect and her anger had faded so she was zapped and in need of family. She said yes to going into town with the couple instead of heading first thing to the mountain.

8.

This town had been named after the palm that flooded the area. The markets were not on. Instead, talk about storm damage. Another coffee in the cafe on the corner and a piece of buttered quinoa bread left on the boy's plate.

She said her goodbyes as her mother might, with humour, with a bit of lingo rolled up in there. She moved on quickly.

There was a bus stop at the servo. Sis sat there – the bus didn't come for an hour. A woman came past and asked how to get to the community by the mountain.

The woman was the mother of one of the young men who had died. She had driven in from the Granite Belt. Her son was gay, she said, living in one of the least tolerant towns in the country. He and his partner lived in fear but could not move because their work was there. They had gone on a road trip for the weekend. The mother of the son could not believe it had stormed overnight. The sun was out and the sky was as the sea. Sis told the mother her ancestors would be in mourning.

9.

Is it hard? Do your legs shake when you don't want them to? Sis asked Donna as they sat on the sand they'd brought up from the beach.

You learn the story for the dance and then it's not so hard. Donna let the red skirt on her waist come around her and mix with the sand.

The centre's doors opened, and the room started filling up. Donna was given her woven band. Other women, young and old, wore these bands around their wrists and ankles.

She said to Donna, When I was younger, I thought white people couldn't see black cockatoos, from Mum.

True?

Yeah, I thought they were invisible to them. And you know, last night, I think I was invisible. Last night I wanna die and I scream and cry and the whitefellas didn't hear me.

And today? Donna looked up from tying the band around her ankle.

Sis helped make space. There were didge and possum skin drums coming. The drums bumped together as they were carried through the space and made the start of a sound.

Today I'm here.

Publication Details

Dominic Amerena's 'Help Me Harden My Heart' appeared in *Australian Book Review* (6 January 2017).

Madeline Bailey's 'The Encyclopaedia of Wild Things' appeared in *Voiceworks* (Issue 106, December 2016).

Tony Birch's 'Sissy' appeared in *Westerly* (Vol. 62, No. 1, July 2017).

Verity Borthwick's 'Barren Ground' appeared in *And Watch the Whale Explode: UTS Writers' Anthology 2017* (NewSouth Books, 2017).

Elizabeth Flux's 'One's Company' appeared in *The Legend of Monga Khan: An Aussie Folk Hero* (Peter Drew Arts, 2016).

Cassie Hamer's 'By Proxy' appeared in *Mascara Literary Review* (Issue 20, April 2017).

John Kinsella's 'The Telephone' appeared in *Southerly*, (Vol. 76, Issue 3, May 2017).

Julie Koh's 'The Wall' appeared in the *Canary Press* (Issue 10, August 2016).

Melissa Lucashenko's 'Dreamers' appeared in *The Near and The Far: New Stories from the Asia-Pacific Region* (Scribe, 2016).

Jennifer Mills's 'Miracles' appeared in *Meanjin* (Vol. 76, Issue 1, Autumn 2017).

Joshua Mostafa's 'The Boat' appeared in *Southerly* (Vol. 76, Issue 3, May 2017).

Ryan O'Neill's 'Polly Stepford (1932–1997)' appeared in *Meanjin* (Vol. 76, Issue 3, Spring 2016).

David Oberg's 'Nose Bleed' appeared in the *Lifted Brow* (Issue 33, March 2017).

Allee Richards's 'Perry Feral' appeared in *Kill Your Darlings* (Issue 29, April 2017).

Mirandi Riwoe's 'Growth' appeared in *Review of Australian Fiction* (Vol. 21, Issue 3, February 2017).

Josephine Rowe's 'Glisk' appeared in *Australian Book Review* (Issue 383, August 2016).

Joe Rubbo's 'Trampoline' appeared in *The Near and The Far: New Stories from the Asia-Pacific Region* (Scribe, 2016).

Beejay Silcox's 'Slut Trouble' appeared in *Australian Book Review* (6 January 2017).

Ellen van Neerven's 'Sis Better' appeared in the *Saturday Paper* (24 December 2016).

Notes on Contributors

The Editor

Maxine Beneba Clarke is an Australian writer and poet of Afro-Caribbean descent. She is the author of the Indie and ABIA award-winning short fiction collection *Foreign Soil* (2014). Her most recent poetry collection, *Carrying the World,* won the 2017 Victorian Premier's Award for Poetry. Maxine is the author of the CBCA-winning picture book *The Patchwork Bike* (a collaboration with Melbourne artist Van T. Rudd), and her critically acclaimed memoir *The Hate Race* is being adapted for stage for Melbourne's Malthouse Theatre. She writes for the *Saturday Paper.*

The Authors

Dominic Amerena is a writer from Melbourne. His work has appeared in places like *Australian Book Review, Overland,* the *Australian,* the *Lifted Brow,* the *Age, Meanjin* and *Kill Your Darlings.* His work has been recognised in a number of awards, most recently the 2017 ABR Elizabeth Jolley Short Story Prize.

Madeline Bailey is a writer, born in Hobart in 1996. She won the 2016 Melbourne Young Writer's Award, has been published in *Voiceworks,* performed at the Wheeler Centre, and is studying at the University of Melbourne.

Tony Birch is the author of *Shadowboxing* (2006), *Father's Day* (2009), *Blood* (2011), *The Promise* (2014), *Ghost River* (2015), *Broken Teeth* (2016) and *Common People* (2017).

Verity Borthwick comes to writing from a background in geology. She spent four years looking at one crystal of salt for her PhD and started writing in her spare time so as not to go mad. She has been published in *Island* and the *UTS Writers' Anthology 2017*.

Raelee Chapman grew up in the Riverina. Her short fiction has been published in *Westerly*, *Southerly* and *Mascara Literary Review*. In 2017 one of her published stories placed as a finalist in *The Best Small Fictions* (US). She currently resides in Singapore with her family.

Elizabeth Flux is a freelance writer and editor. She was the winner of the inaugural Feminartsy Fiction Prize and recently completed a Wheeler Centre Hot Desk Fellowship. Her nonfiction work has been widely published, and includes essays on film, pop culture, feminism and identity.

Cassie Hamer is a Sydney-based writer whose short works have been published by *Mascara Literary Review*, *Margaret River Press* and *Writer's Edit*. She has been shortlisted and placed in a number of writing competitions, and in 2017 won the Shoalhaven Literary Award.

John Kinsella has published six volumes of short stories, most recently *Old Growth* (Transit Lounge, 2017). He is Professor of Literature and Environment at Curtin University and a Fellow of Churchill College, Cambridge University.

Julie Koh (許瑩玲) is the author of *Capital Misfits* and *Portable Curiosities*, which was shortlisted for the Readings Prize for New Australian Fiction, the Steele Rudd Award and a NSW Premier's Literary Award. Her fiction has appeared in *The Best Australian Stories* (2014–2016) and *Best Australian Comedy Writing*. She is a 2017 *Sydney Morning Herald* Best Young Australian Novelist and a founding member of Kanganoulipo.

Melissa Lucashenko is a multi-award-winning Goorie novelist and essayist. Her work is about a better Australia for all.

Myfanwy McDonald is a Melbourne-based writer of fiction. Her stories have been published in the *Big Issue, Going Down Swinging* and *Tincture.* 'Numb' was shortlisted for the 2017 Commonwealth Short Story Prize. myfanwy-mcdonald.squarespace.com

Jennifer Mills is the author of the novels *Gone* and *The Diamond Anchor* and the short story collection *The Rest Is Weight.* Her next novel, *Dyschronia*, will be published by Picador in February 2018.

Joshua Mostafa is a doctoral candidate at the Writing and Society Centre, Western Sydney University. His creative practice explores the interstices of prose and formal poetry, narrative and the lyric, and of the written and the spoken word. He lives in the Blue Mountains.

Ryan O'Neill is a short story writer. His latest book, *Their Brilliant Careers: The Fantastic Lives of Sixteen Extraordinary Australian Writers*, was shortlisted for the 2017 Miles Franklin Award. He is a founding member of the Australian experimental writing group Kanganoulipo.

David Oberg is a Brisbane-based writer whose work has been published in the *Lifted Brow.*

Allee Richards is a playwright and fiction writer from Melbourne. Her stories have been published in the *Lifted Brow, Kill Your Darlings* and *Voiceworks.*

Mirandi Riwoe's debut novel is *She Be Damned* (Pantera Press, Legend Press) and her novella *The Fish Girl* won *Seizure*'s Viva la Novella competition. Her work has appeared in *Review of Australian Fiction, Rex, Peril* and *Shibboleth and Other Stories.* Mirandi has a PhD in creative writing and literary studies.

Josephine Rowe is the author of two story collections and a novel, *A Loving, Faithful Animal* (UQP, 2016). She holds fellowships from the Wallace Stegner program at Stanford University and the International Writing Program at the University of Iowa. She currently lives in Tasmania.

Joe Rubbo lives in Melbourne, where he works as a full-time bookseller. He is a 2015 WrICE fellow.

Beejay Silcox has been kicked in the head by a gorilla, blessed by a voodoo priest, and stuck in quicksand; she eloped to Las Vegas, and drove to Timbuktu in a car held together with a bra-strap. She recently completed her MFA, and works as a writer and literary critic.

Ellen van Neerven is the award-winning author of *Heat and Light* (UQP, 2014) and *Comfort Food* (UQP, 2016).